Charlotte Campbell Bury

The Exclusives

Vol. 2

Charlotte Campbell Bury

The Exclusives
Vol. 2

ISBN/EAN: 9783337363659

Printed in Europe, USA, Canada, Australia, Japan

Cover: Foto ©Andreas Hilbeck / pixelio.de

More available books at **www.hansebooks.com**

THE
EXCLUSIVES.
VOL. II.

THE

EXCLUSIVES.

IN THREE VOLUMES.

VOL. II.

SECOND EDITION.

LONDON:

HENRY COLBURN AND RICHARD BENTLEY,

NEW BURLINGTON STREET.

1830.

LONDON:
Printed by J. L. Cox, Great Queen Street,
Lincoln's-Inn Fields.

THE EXCLUSIVES.

CHAPTER I.

THE CLOSING SCENE AT RESTORMEL.

ON the evening previous to Lord Albert's departure, while Mr. Foley and Lady Hamlet Vernon were intently engaged in playing at chess, Lord Albert announced to Lady Ellersby his intention of leaving Restormel, and paid her the usual compliment of thanks for the honour she had done him in inviting him there.

"You have lost your queen," cried Mr. Foley, addressing Lady Hamlet Vernon, "now in two moves I will give you checkmate, lady fair. But see—what is the matter?—she is ill —she faints—lend assistance for heaven's sake!" Lord Albert flew towards the spot, and caught Lady Hamlet as she was falling to the ground. The usual remedies were applied; and when sufficiently recovered, the sufferer was carried to her room, apparently still unable to speak.

"I hate all scene-makers," said Lady Boileau; "if there is a thing I cannot bear, it is the getting up of a sentimental catastrophe.—Don't you, Mr. Leslie Winyard?—Don't you think it is the acmé of bad taste?"

"Oh! most undoubtedly; nothing argues a decided *roturièrism* more than allowing your feelings, if *real*, to get the better of you in public; and if feigned, nothing is so easily seen through as counterfeiting them, therefore, either way, it is at best a *mistake*."

"One don't look well when one faints—that is to say, *really* faints," observed Lady Ellersby; "it is surely best to avoid doing so."

"One may always command one's-self," observed Lady Baskerville.

"Oh!" said Lady Tilney, who now and then really thought and felt right, "it is very easy to distinguish between a *feint* and a *faint*; and I believe every body would ridicule the first, and nobody would like to do the latter; because, as Lady Ellersby observes, no real fainting, or crying, or any of the convulsions produced by the feelings, are the least graceful, except in the *beau idéal* of a Magdalen, or on a painter's easel; and secondly, because nothing is less likely to produce interest than these kind of physical causes; for, as some great author says, 'all physical sufferings are soon forgotten even by the sufferer, when they are past, and by our friends certainly never remembered beyond their immediate duration, if so long;' consequently I believe Lady Hamlet Vernon did faint *tout bonnement*: she had probably *une indigestion*; poor Lady!—but she will soon be well again."

"Spoken like an orator," said Mr. Spencer Newcombe; "and not only an orator, but a philosopher."

"Par drivers moyens on arrive à pareille fin," said the Comtesse Leinsengen; "and providing one does what one wants to do, that is all that *sinifies*. One person faints, another talks, another dresses, another writes, all in order to get what they wish. On the success depends the wisdom of the measure."

"Agreed," cried Mr. Spencer Newcombe, "and conceived like a *diplomate du premier grade*," he whispered to Lady Baskerville; then aloud, "if Tonnerre had been here he would have said—"

"I will bet you ten to one," cried Mr. Leslie Winyard, "that Lord Albert D'Esterre does not leave Restormel to-morrow."

10

"Done," said Mr. Spencer Newcombe. —

"Done," said Lord Baskerville; "ten to one he does; for I never knew a more obstinate fellow in my life; one who prizes himself more *on decision of character*—and when he says he will do a thing he will do it, however little he may like the thing when done."

"I don't think he will go," said Lady Ellersby, gently.

"Why not?" asked Lady Tilney.

"Lady Hamlet Vernon will not let him."

"C'est tout simple," rejoined Comtesse Leinsengen, with a shrug of her shoulders.

"It appears to me," said Lady Baskerville, "that if he does go he will not be very much missed. I never knew so dull a member of society; he never speaks but to lay down the law, or to inculcate some moral truth: now really when one has done with the nursery, that is rather too bad."

"Providing she don't drive away George Foley," said Lady Boileau, "she may reap the fruits of her fainting here."

"Mr. Foley," replied Lady Baskerville to her dear friend, "is the man in the world who will do whatever suits him best; and I particularly admire *his* manner and his ways: they are all perfectly in good taste; and I have already promised him that he shall be my *cavaliere servente* for the season."

"Promised!—well, dear Lady Baskerville, I thought you were too prudent to make such promises. What will Lord Baskerville say?" lowering her tone to a whisper.

Lady Baskerville, speaking aloud—"Oh, dear! la! I should never have thought of asking him what he likes upon such an occasion;—we live too well together to trouble each other with our little arrangements.—Is it not true, Lord Baskerville? do we not do exactly as we choose?"

"I hope your Ladyship does," he replied, in all the airs of his exclusive character; "I should conceive myself vastly unhappy if you did not?" Lady Baskerville looked significantly at her dear friend Lady Boileau; who knew, as well as herself, that this ultra-liberalism of her Lord in regard to the conduct of wives, whatever it might be in respect to husbands, was entirely assumed on Lord Baskerville's part.

While this conversation passed in the drawing-room, Lord Albert and Mr. Foley were discoursing in their apartment above-stairs. They had each expressed great interest about Lady Hamlet Vernon's indisposition; and after waiting some time to hear accounts of her from her female attendants, they fell into other conversation of various kinds, during which Lord Albert D'Esterre found himself unfeignedly amused and interested with the talents, taste, and refinement of Mr. Foley; and the more so, as he spoke much of Dunmelraise and its inhabitants, and was lavish in his praise of Lady Adeline.

"There is only one point," he said, "which however is hardly worth mentioning, for of course it only arises out of the seclusion and the monotony of her present existence; but certainly Lady Adeline, *pour trancher le mot*, is a *little* methodistical—the sooner you go and put that matter to rights the better." Lord Albert's manner of receiving the latter part of this information, proved to Mr. Foley that he had mistaken the character of the person he addressed, and he added,

"But indeed Lady Adeline Seymour is so perfect, that it matters very little what she does—every thing *she does* must be right."—The conversation then took another turn, and they parted.

Lord Albert D'Esterre was not what might be called a

jealous man; but no man, no human being can be without the possibility of feeling jealousy—neither was he naturally suspicious, but nothing is more apt to generate a suspicion of the fidelity of another's conduct, than the consciousness of any breach in the integrity of our own. He pressed his hand to his heart—he sat down—rose up—paced his chamber, and still repeated to himself the praises which Mr. Foley had uttered of *his* Adeline. "*My* Adeline," he said, and then again stopped; "but is she *mine*? do I deserve she should still be *mine*, when I have so neglected her? no!"—His servant came into the room with a note, the well known shape and colour of which he could not mistake. It was placed in his hand—he opened it carelessly and was about to cast it away, when the name of *Adeline* caught his eye; then he hastily read the following words.

"It is not for myself I mourn—it is not the threatened loss of your society, however much I value it, which has occasioned my being so overpowered—it is the knowledge of a secret which pertains to another, and in which your fate is involved, that has quite mastered me—this much I must tell you. I must see you before you go, I must prepare you for your meeting with Lady Adeline Seymour." Twenty times he read over this note. "What can it mean? can its meaning be that Adeline loves Mr. Foley, at least that he thinks so? and I, what have I been doing? into what a sea of troubles have I plunged for the enjoyment of the society of a person that in fact affords me none—for the empty speculation of recalling the chaotic mind of one (comparatively a stranger to me) to a sense of reason and religion, fool that I was for the attempt." Then, after a considerable pause, and after deep reflection, he burst forth:

"Prepare *me* for a meeting with Adeline!" as his eye caught again the last line of the note. "*Prepare me for a meeting with Adeline*—I cannot bear the phrase; but I must know what

13

she means—I must drag this secret from her:"—and he rang the bell violently!—"I shall not want my horses till one o'clock instead of seven to-morrow morning."

The night Lord Albert passed was one of feverish anxiety. He sent to inquire for Lady Hamlet Vernon at an early hour the next day; and hearing she was much recovered, he besought her to grant the interview she had done him the favour to offer as soon as she possibly could. She replied, that in that house it would be reckoned a breach of all decorum, if she received him at any undue hour; but that as soon as the earliest part of the company breakfasted, which was about one o'clock, she would be sure, notwithstanding her indisposition, to be in the breakfast-room at that time; when she would avail herself of some opportunity to give him the information which had come to her knowledge. This short delay seemed an age to him. Every one knows, when suspense agitates the mind, what a total anarchy ensues, and the hours which intervened before meeting Lady Hamlet Vernon seemed to Lord Albert interminable. When they *did* meet, the intervening moments ere an opportunity occurred of Lord Albert's drawing her aside, appeared in their turn so many more ages of suffering.

At last the company rose from the breakfast table, and as Lady Hamlet took Lord Albert's arm, and walked out on the terrace under the window, she said, "This is kind of you to have listened to my request:" and then as they walked from the house, proceeded in a graver tone to add, "I am aware, dear Lord Albert, that my note of last night must have surprised you, and that the subject connected with it, on which I am about to touch, is one of the utmost delicacy, and one which upon the very verge of the attempt I shrink from; but you have evinced so much real interest in the state of my wayward mind, and have said so much to me with a view, I am certain, of placing my happiness on a more secure

14

and steady foundation than I had ever any chance of before, that I should be ungrateful in the extreme, if a corresponding wish for your comfort in life did not in turn actuate me. I cannot be ignorant of the engagement between yourself and Lady Adeline Seymour, the fulfilment of which will not, I presume, be long delayed; unless, indeed—"

Here Lady Hamlet Vernon's voice faltered, and for a moment she paused; but, as if making an effort to subdue her emotion, she added in a lower and firmer tone, and with an expression of something like intreaty in her countenance as she looked up at Lord Albert, "Unless I, dear Lord Albert, shall prove the happy instrument of saving you from too precipitate a step in this matter. May I continue to speak to you thus unreservedly?" Lord Albert made no answer, but bowed his head in token of assent, while he walked by her side like one lost in a perturbed dream. She continued,

"I wished, before you went, for this opportunity, because I was aware that it was the only one left in which what I am about to impart would ever be of use; for, lovely as Lady Adeline is, possessed of charms of person which would indeed draw any heart towards her, of the warmest and most enthusiastic disposition, deeply enamoured of *you* as well as sacredly alive to her engagement to you (and I know her, from a source which cannot mislead me, in person, in mind, in heart, and in determination, to be all that I describe to you)—how could even your judgment, Lord Albert, which is stronger than many of twice your years, but yield to such united influence, and be tempted to decide at the moment on making so much perfection irrevocably your own. But with all these transcendant charms of person and of character, Lady Adeline, I am grieved to say, and know, has been unhappily betrayed into views of life and of the world, which must unfit her to be the partner of any one who does not think in accordance with her on these subjects. From what cause or under what influence the peculiar turn of mind she has taken has arisen, I know not, but (and again I must repeat, that I *know* the too-sure truth of all I say) it has been gradually and fearfully on the increase, and is now become a fixed principle with her.

"She loves *you*, as I have said, and she looks upon the coming union with you as the fulfilment of a sacred engagement, and a duty she has to perform; but with this she views the rank you hold in society, and in which she will be associated, only imposing on herself obligations of a higher and severer order, and calling for a stricter conduct and a greater self-denial on her part. She condemns what she calls the dissipations and wicked employment of time, in the world of fashion; she holds dress, beyond the plainest attire, to be a misapplication of the gifts of fortune; she laments over the worldly career of any one whom she hears talked of with applause, or whose talents raise them to distinction in the public eye: she has even, I understand, wholly abandoned her music and her drawing, as too alluring and dangerous an occupation, wasting the time which ought to be devoted to serious reading, and an acquirement of that spirit which has already cast such a gloom over her existence. The only active employment in which she indulges herself beyond her books, is in making clothes for and visiting the poor in her mother's domain. In short, she is what the world calls a methodist, a saint; I know not exactly what these words mean, but I know they are terms applied by people of sense to an ultraism in religious matters."

Lord Albert shuddered, and a sigh was the only interruption he gave, as Lady Hamlet proceeded.

"Conceive yourself, my dear Lord Albert, united to a person of this character, however amiable in herself, with your talents, with your views, which are" (and she looked at him steadily as she spoke) "tinctured with ambition. With your temper and your tastes for the elegancies of life, how would you brook a wife who was praying and singing psalms all day long? who would consider all *your* actions, when not in accordance with her own, as so many positive sins, and whose moments, such at least as were spared from the offices of her enthusiasm, would be passed in the cottages of your tenants, and in making baby-linen for every expected increase in their families.

"Now let me beseech you, and believe me to speak from the most disinterested feelings, that when you meet Lady Adeline, you will not betray yourself into a too hasty arrangement for your union. See her—see her, by all means. Judge for yourself; use your own eyes, hear with your own ears, and be the arbiter of your own cause, but do nothing rashly. Time is necessary for all decisions in momentous questions; and what can be more momentous, and in what is there more at stake, than in an union for life? Can too much deliberation be given to the subject? Alas! I know, from my own fatal experience, what misery must ensue where no tastes, no principles, no objects exist in common between those united. I owe to this cause a great portion of my present unhappiness; for the misery I endured, and the constant efforts I made to bear up against the tenfold wretchedness of my marriage with Lord Hamlet Vernon, impaired my intellectual powers, and prevented my turning the energies of my mind to any useful or profitable purpose. Hence I have become what I am, dependant on the resources of the hour, to enable me to pass through life with any thing like composure."

Lord Albert had listened with feelings which it would be impossible to describe to all that had fallen from Lady Hamlet Vernon; and in the emotion, which her communication and her entreaties produced, he could find no words for utterance, no answer to her appeals. He was like one dumb, and deprived of sense; and he stood for some moments rooted to the spot when the voice of his counsellor had ceased.

"See her! yes, I will see my Adeline," he at length said in a deep agonized tone, as if communing with himself. "Yes, I will see her."

"Lord Albert, I entreat you, I implore you," cried Lady Hamlet Vernon, with an emotion that made her words quiver on her lips, "I beseech you forgive me, if'—the window of the library was at this moment thrown hastily up; and Lord Albert D'Esterre heard his name called by Lord Ellersby, who held in his hand a letter.

"D'Esterre," said he, "here are your letters." Lord Albert hastened forward mechanically to receive them, and one he gazed upon more intently than the rest, as he looked them over—it was from Adeline.

Who is there who has not recognised, even in its peculiar folding, the letter of a beloved object? and whose heart has not throbbed with delight ere even the seal were broken? Such was the emotion of Lord Albert, awoke up from the paralyzing influence of Lady Hamlet Vernon's communication to new life by the letter he now pressed to his bosom; and regardless of what had passed, he hastened to his room, and read as follows:—

"DEAREST:—My mother has been gradually growing worse and worse these two months, and I have persuaded her to go to town for a consultation of her physicians.

"It is so long since I have heard from you, Albert, it is painful for me to write, scarcely knowing how far you may be interested in what I have to communicate—but

18

I try to still my uneasiness—let me but see you, dear Albert, all will be forgotten, all will be forgiven; for I am your own true and affectionate

"ADELINE."

"P.S. You will find us at Mamma's house in town."

A letter like this, breathing such trust and love, and so replete with genuine expression of delight in the prospect of meeting him, was indeed sufficient to make Lord Albert forget at once the poisonous theme which his ears rather than his reason had imbibed in his interview with Lady Hamlet. Impelled more by the eager anxiety of affection to behold the object of his late disquietude, than to see her for the purpose of convincing himself of her errors, he leapt with alacrity into his carriage, and drove towards London, without casting a thought on those he left behind.

The mortification which Lady Hamlet Vernon felt was severe, in proportion as from its nature it admitted of no sympathy. She was, of course, ignorant of the cause of Lord Albert's destination being so suddenly changed from Wales to London; but in the blindness of her increasing passion, she resolved in the first moment of her despair to follow him thither. A cooler judgment, however, made her recollect that if she lost Lord Albert she had other friends to retain, a position in the gay world to lose, and that, at all events, it was not by pursuing him at that moment that any thing was to be gained; she therefore determined on remaining some days at Restormel, and making herself as agreeable as possible to the party that continued there. To one of Lady Hamlet Vernon's disposition this was no easy task. Violent and impetuous as she was by nature, left as she had been without any control, it was a very Herculean work to hide all the warring passions of jealousy and disappointed love beneath the semblance of a cool indifference—a disengaged mind.

"What have you done with Lord Albert?" was Lady Baskerville's first question to her after the morning's salutation; "I hear he departed in violent haste at an undue hour this morning. He looks of such an imperturbable gravity, one does not understand his ever being brought to do any thing out of measure or rule."

"I done with Lord Albert? my dear Lady Baskerville, you confer too much honour upon me to suppose that *I* have any influence with him. I did not even know that he was gone; but if you are very much interested in his departure, perhaps Lord Ellersby can tell us something about it."

She thought by this means to discover the cause of his sudden disappearance, and gratify her inquiries as being the curiosity of another.—"Lord Ellersby," she said, "Lady Baskerville is desirous to learn what wonderful event can have called Lord Albert away from us so very suddenly."

"I do not know," said Lord Ellersby, "unless he is going to be prime minister; don't you think, Winyard, he has the dignity of office on his brows already?"

"In his own opinion, I make no doubt, he stands a fair chance for the highest situations; but we have quite exploded all that sort of fudge now-a-days, and I think, unless we were to have a bare-bone parliament, and a cabinet of puritans, his very consequential lordship has not much prospect of success in that line."

"No," said Lady Tenderden, taking up a newspaper, "I think this paragraph in the Morning Post will rather explain the secret of Lord Albert's going away:—

"'We understand Lady Dunmelraise, with her beautiful daughter Lady Adeline Seymour, is shortly expected in town, and are sorry to add that Lady Dunmelraise's ill health has hitherto caused her absence from the gay circles of fashion.'—This is put in by herself, or some of her friends, you may depend upon it."

"Dear," said Lady Baskerville, "those vulgar newspapers are always filled with trash of that sort; nobody attends to such nonsense. I dare say this Lady Adeline is some awkward raw girl, enough to make one shiver to think of; however, she may do very well as a wife for Lord Albert, and he may be gone to meet her."

"Oh, I do assure you," cried Lady Tilney, "that the public papers are the vehicles of a great deal of good or evil; and that not only political discussion, but the discussion also of the affairs of individuals, is constantly promoted by the freedom of the press."

"For my part," said Lady Baskerville, "I think it is quite abominable that those vulgar editors of newspapers should be allowed to comment upon what we do."

"Not at all, my dear Lady Baskerville; allow me to assure you that we are much more known—much more distinguished—much more *répandus* by being all named occasionally, never mind how or in what manner, in the public papers. Besides, on the freedom of the press hangs all the law and the prophets; and if some few suffer by it occasionally, the multitude are gainers; and I can never repine at the glorious spirit of public liberty which the papers and the press maintain. Don't you agree with me, Lord Ellersby?"

"I like it all very well when it does not interfere with me," he replied, yawning; "but I think it is very disagreeable when these vulgar fellows, the news-writers, say some impertinent thing, for which I cannot give them a rap over the knuckles."

"La, what does it signify," rejoined Lady Ellersby; "nobody thinks of any thing above a very few days, and except some dear friend or other, no person of good breeding mentions the subject to one, if it be disagreeable, so that I cannot really say it disturbs my tranquillity for a moment, let them say what they will. As to this puff about Lady Adeline Seymour, I agree with Lady Baskerville, there are always a set of would-be fashionables, who pay for the putting in of such paragraphs about themselves, *et l'on sait parfaitement à quoi s'en tenir* respecting them."

"Nevertheless," rejoined Mr. Foley, who had just laid down his book, "I do assure you that, puff or no puff, Lady Adeline Seymour will astonish you all, for she is a very extraordinary person."

"Then I am sure I shall not be able to suffer her," said Lady Baskerville.

"*Je déteste les phénomènes*," said Comtesse Leinsengen.

"Mr. Foley seems to be paid too," rejoined Lady Tenderden, laughing, "for making the young lady notorious; and we shall see him with a placard stuck on his shoulders, setting forth the beauties and perfections of the wonderful young lady."

"These *miracles*," cried Comtesse Leinsengen, "are only fit to be shewn for half-a-crown a piece; if you interest yourself very much in her benefit, remember, I promise to take tickets."

Mr. Foley smiled as, he replied: "I shall leave it to time to prove to every one of you how very much you are mistaken."

"By all that is romantic," cried Mr. Winyard, "Foley is caught at last; he is positively going to become a lackadaisical swain, and write sonnets to his mistress's eyebrows."

"Perhaps even so. It is amusing to take up a new character now and then; it is like changing the air, and is equally beneficial to the health, moral and physical. Nothing so fatiguing as being always the same, both for the sake of one's-self, as well as of our associates—don't you think so, Mr. Winyard?"

"I have always shewn that I did so think. Few persons have acted up to their principles in this respect more conscientiously than myself." Mr. Foley did not press this matter further; he knew when to retire from the field, and always cautiously avoided a defeat. This conversation was at once a key to Lady Hamlet Vernon, and much as it pleased her to have discovered the truth, she resolved to carry on the deception; but Lady Hamlet Vernon felt that her total silence might be construed into an interest which, however real, she by no means wished should appear to exist in its true colours, and therefore she forced herself into saying, with apparent indifference, "I understand Lord Albert D'Esterre's marriage is shortly to take place; and whatever people may do *after* marriage, they must be a little attentive *beforehand*; so I doubt not that the arrival of Lady Dunmelraise in town is really the cause which has deprived us of his society; and you know I am one of those who hazard a favourable opinion of Lord Albert, notwithstanding Lady Baskerville's dissentient voice."

This speech she conceived to be one of unprejudiced tone and feeling that would lull all suspicion to rest, had any existed, as to the nature of her real sentiments; and it at least prevented the expression of that ridicule, which would otherwise have been her portion. In this society there was a general system of deceiving on the one hand, and detecting on the other, which constituted its chief entertainment and business; and in the present instance it formed, as usual, one of the main springs of the interest that filled up the remaining hours spent by the party at Restormel.

CHAPTER II.

THE BRIDE'S RETURN.

The approaching gaieties of London, after Easter, were pronounced likely to be of a more brilliant description than they had been for years, as is always the case, according to the interests and wishes of the persons who raise the report. One of the earliest arrivals in the scene of *ton* was that of the Glenmores, who had returned from Paris, whither they had proceeded, it will be remembered, shortly after their marriage.

London, however, was still empty; a considerable part of the *élite* remained at Restormel, and others of their corps were not yet reunited; while such as had in fact nothing to do with them, were nevertheless sufficiently foolish to regulate their movements by those of the exclusives.

It was in this interval between the two assignable points of a London season that Lord Glenmore, turning the corner into the still deserted region of Hyde Park, met there, to his surprise, Lord Albert D'Esterre, who sat his horse like one careless of what was passing around him, and seemingly so absorbed in his own thoughts, that the exercise of riding had the appearance at that moment with him of a mechanical habit, rather than a thing of choice. So deeply occupied was he in reflection, that Lord Glenmore was obliged to call several times, and at length to ride close up to him, before he could attract his attention.

"D'Esterre," said he, as he held out his hand, "I rejoice to meet you; and this unexpected pleasure is the greater, as I thought you had been too fashionable a man to be yet in London, at least for a day or two to come. But how ill you look! what is the matter with you?"

Lord Albert was not in a mood to bear interruption from any one, or exactly able, without putting a force upon himself, to meet any inquiry with a courteous answer. But Lord Glenmore was, perhaps, one of the very few exceptions in whose favour something of this feeling was abated, for their intimacy had been of long standing; and Lord Albert's regard and respect for his character was, as it deserved to be, of the highest kind.

As soon, therefore, as the latter was roused from his reverie by the kindly voice of his friend, he greeted him with answering warmth, and inquired after Lady Glenmore with that cordial interest which he felt for the wife of his friend; he at the same time endeavoured to laugh off Lord Glenmore's observations on his own personal appearance, which were nevertheless well-founded—for his mind was labouring under an anxiety which visibly displayed itself in his countenance, and which, as his first emotion of pleasure in the near prospect of meeting Lady Adeline subsided, the mysterious words of Lady Hamlet Vernon's note were too well calculated to give rise to. This state of uneasiness was by no means diminished by the delay of Lady Dunmelraise's arrival in town. At her house Lord Albert's hourly inquiries had for two days been fruitless; and he was returning from South Audley Street, with the expression of increased disappointment painted in his looks, when he met Lord Glenmore.

After some conversation of a general nature, and inquiries into the events which had arisen in the fashionable world during his absence, and which the latter confessed himself to have been too happy to have thought about before, he asked Lord D'Esterre, with a manner implying more interest, what were his own views and intentions.

"I hope you are not thinking of returning abroad," he added, "for we want you at home, and then you must marry." Lord Albert sighed as his friend approached the subject so near his heart, but which he was little inclined to discuss with him at that particular moment; while the other, without remarking the grave expression that had returned over Lord Albert's countenance, continued: —

"Allow me to speak to you as a man who has lived a little longer in the world than yourself, and to whom you formerly communicated what were your views and wishes in life. You told me you would aim at diplomacy and at office; I am sure in both from noble motives, and because you felt it to be your bias, which in all our pursuits is half the battle in ensuring success. Now you must permit me to tell you that, however great or powerful in point of interest a man may be, he can never with these objects be too much of the latter. Above all things, then, keep this principle before you; and, in any alliance that you may form (for you will marry soon, depend upon it: the ladies, if there were no fears from yourself, will not allow you to remain long in single blessedness), endeavour to remember my advice, and look round you before you take the leap which is to break the neck of your liberty, and do not throw away the advantages which your situation (to say nothing of yourself) give you of selecting where you choose, and where you think your pursuits will best be promoted.

"Now there is one, *par parenthèse*, among the many desirable parties I could name to you—which is Osbaldeston's daughter. His interest is great; but he has taken through life the most foolish of all parts in politics—that of being of neither party; and, as an independent peer, is alternately hated and caressed, abused and praised, despised and sought after by both. You know, since the death of his eldest son, all his affections centre in this daughter; and I am persuaded that any one united to her, may make all Lord Osbaldeston's interests his own. I do not mean to force this match upon you," smiling as he spoke; "but I allude to it as a sample of what, as your friend, and one thinking with you in politics, and pretty much the same in all other matters, and having your interest, my dear D'Esterre, much at heart, I would rejoice to see you assent to. *Enfin*—the Osbaldestons dine with us to-day, and if you will join us, you will have an opportunity of judging for yourself."

Lord Albert, as if he thought himself doomed to undergo violence on all sides in regard to Lady Adeline, replied with more petulance in the tone of his voice than he was ever known to give way to—

"My dear friend, you forget that I am an engaged man."

"Oh, if you mean to allude to Lady Adeline Seymour, I had understood that it was only that sort of engagement which might be dissolved or not, as the parties chose when they came to years of discretion; and as I had heard it whispered that Lady Adeline was attached to a young man who was much at Dunmelraise, and a *protégé* of her mother's, a certain Mr. George Foley, who turned all the women's heads about two years ago in London (Lady Hamlet Vernon's among the rest, by the way), I could not suppose, seeing you very quietly here, that your heart was much engaged; and I thought I knew you too well to believe that you would ever marry (however much I hope you will make a prudent alliance) where love and esteem do not constitute a part of the compact."

"My dear Glenmore, I see your kind intention, through this apparent carelessness of my feelings; but allow me to assure you, you are misinformed—a purer, truer, or more innocent creature does not exist than Lady Adeline Seymour; and though I have been separated lately from her, yet from my correspondence with herself, and from the invariable accounts I have received from others, I feel assured that the ingenuousness of her character would never allow her to have a thought concealed from her mother or myself in the momentous question between us. Oh no; when I look back to her every letter, the recollection brings conviction along with it of her heart being unchanged."

Lord Albert spoke with an inward agitation which corresponded little with the confidence which his words expressed. His outward appearance, however, was calm; and Lord Glenmore, supposing he had been led into a very pardonable error, and wholly innocent of intentionally wounding his friend's feelings, proceeded—

"Well, if it is thus, D'Esterre, you are already a married man, I conceive; but be it so, that does not prevent your dining with me to-day—pray come."

Lord Albert declined, saying gravely, "no! that cannot be; for I am in hourly expectation of Lady Adeline's arrival with her mother, who, I am sorry to add, comes to town on account of her health." A momentary pause ensued in the conversation; and Lord Albert, seemingly little inclined to renew the last topic or enter upon any new one, seized the opportunity of bidding his companion farewell, and they separated.

From the somewhat cold and reserved manner of his parting, Lord Glenmore, when alone, began to think he had committed a mistake in treating his friend's engagement with Lady Adeline lightly, and condemned himself for what had escaped him on the subject. For Lord Glenmore was a man of honourable, as well as kindly feelings; and in giving the counsel of a *prudential* marriage to Lord Albert, was at the same time the last person to think that, in an union for life, happiness ought to be sacrificed to interested views: the furthest also from his thoughts would have been any design to interfere between, or to disunite any two persons who were attached to each other. Perhaps the world in general might not have given him credit for this amiability of feeling, or for the strict principle which he really possessed, from seeing that he lived in constant intercourse with a class, where, if similar worth of character did exist at all, it certainly never was looked up to as a merit in the possessor. It must be allowed that Lord Glenmore was any thing rather than a fitting member of such a class; for in addition to warmth of heart, natural affection, and good principles, he possessed talents of a very superior kind, and held opinions quite at variance with the received creed of his companions.

He believed, for instance, that life was given for other purposes than to be spent in accident alone, or that a perpetual course of frivolous pursuits, without any higher aim or object, should be suffered to govern human existence; but that, on the contrary, every action should tend to some useful purpose. If Lord Glenmore was ambitious (and he was so), his ambition was of a noble kind; and while he sought power, his uprightness of character could never suffer him to abuse its exercise. He was called proud by some: but although impressed with a sense of the dignity of the aristocracy to which he belonged, it was not a blind and foolish estimate of rank which made him value it, but a conviction of the importance and responsibility which every one placed in the higher grades of society possesses, while fulfilling the duties of the sphere in which Providence places him; and if in society he sometimes appeared reserved, and joined not in all the empty, uninteresting topics that make up the conversation of most of the coteries of *ton*, it was—that his mind was filled, even in the buzz of the vapid talk around him, with matters worthy of the reflection and study of an intellectual being.

He owed his admission, consequently, within the line of circumvallation drawn by the *ultra* leaders of fashion, to a dread of the important consequence of his remaining aloof from their circle, and the preponderating influence which even his neutrality would afford (for Lord Glenmore was not a man to lend himself to either side in such a frivolous warfare as the decision of who were, or who were not, worthy members of the *corps élite*). Although the exclusives, therefore, one and all, considered him to fall short of a due proportion of that species of merit necessary to their order, yet still they united in one common effort to retain him on their side. They could have wished him, no doubt, allied to one of their own peculiar choosing, and had heard with dismay proportionate to the consequences which might frustrate their plans respecting him, the announcement of his marriage with his present wife.

Determined, however, to make the best of the unpropitious event, they had from the first decided on the general policy of endeavouring to retain Lord Glenmore's influence, by admitting Lady Glenmore (however much she might be considered inadmissible) amongst them; and thus to secure in the opinion of the world the sanction of her husband to live on terms of intimacy in their set.

It was this motive which in some degree influenced the ladies who were present at Lady Melcomb's ball, and subsequently at the marriage, to risk the loss of *caste* by being seen in the motley collection of that lady's assembly: though the ties of relationship, in one or two instances, would have led them to the re-union on such a happy occasion. Yet with Lady Ellersby and Lady Tenderden these were impulses, which were only to be acted upon when the laws and dogmas of exclusiveness permitted such a proceeding.

When Lord Glenmore returned from the Continent with his young bride, the news of his arrival quickly spread through the exclusive circle, and called for some decisive measure on their part, to ascertain how he might be induced still to remain, under the circumstances of his new connexion, in the same degree of intimacy with them. It was therefore time, on the part of the exclusives, for bringing to bear these intentions at the moment of their re-assembling in London, and more particularly on that of the individuals who composed the party at Restormel.

Lady Tilney, whose activity was ever on the alert, ordered her carriage before the morning show of London began, that she might catch all the chiefs of her party at home. The first house she visited was Lady Ellersby's, who was not yet risen, but she was admitted to her bed-side.

"*Reveillez-vous belle endormie*," said Lady Tilney, kissing her on both sides of her face, "for what do you think I am come about?"

"I cannot imagine: has Lady Hamlet Vernon gone off with any body, or do the ministry totter, or has Newmarket proved unsuccessful, or, in short, tell me what *has* happened!"

"No, my dear, nothing of all that; but the Glenmores are come back from Paris, and now or never must the question be ultimately decided whether we are to retain Lord Glenmore amongst us or not. You know we were agreed on the general policy of doing so soon after his marriage, and the first step to take will be to tutor the young Georgina, so that she may not on the outset of her *début* do any thing to

32

disgrace us. But although I considered the matter as settled, I would not take any decided step till I consulted you. It is on this account I am come at so early an hour, lest we should not have acted in concert on this point; for as I always say, it is the disagreement in the cabinet between their own members which always breaks up the administration; so society is, or ought to be, precisely a type of the government of a state: don't you agree with me?"

"Perfectly," replied Lady Ellersby, suppressing a yawn, for she did not, to do her justice, understand one word of the political jargon in which her friend always talked, whether the conversation ran on the choice of a new cap or the admission of a new member to their society. Lady Tilney observing her dear friend's absence of mind, told her that she looked so beautiful in her night-cap, she quite made her forget her errand.

"But, nevertheless," (she added) "I must remind you, that it *is* one of no small importance, for you see what a vast field of interests the Glenmore himself includes. There are the Melcombs, and the D'Esterres, and the Osbaldestons—a perfect host. *Some* of them may play a card in politics: *all* of them are good tools, and I promised Lord Tilney not to lose sight of that consideration. So if we exclude la petite Glenmore, we shall be incurring great risks; whereas, by making her *one of us*, we shall have a vast addition of strength added to our party, and we can always take care that the vulgars belonging to her, who are only good for certain uses, shall not come in her train."

Lady Ellersby, whose attention had been effectually awakened by the admiration of her night-cap, now sat up in her bed and said, "Ah! there indeed is the difficulty—how will you manage that?"

"Nothing easier: we will, as I said, explain to her what an

advantage it is to belong to us, and the necessity of our confining our members to a very small circle, and then tell her that we will always let her know whom she is to invite to her parties, and whom she is to go out with. Thus we shall take care that, from the very beginning, she does not *compromise* us. One or other of us must always be at her right hand, and by flattering Lord Glenmore, and endeavouring to make him believe that Lord Tilney is wavering, and may possibly come round to his side in politics, we shall easily get that sort of power established with both, which it is quite necessary to obtain if they are to belong to us; and that they are so to do is, as I have already explained to you, equally necessary. Not that I, for the world, would make any body do what he did not like to do: no one is more for perfect freedom, as you well know, than myself, but you must feel that not to belong to us, is in fact to be nobody, so that we are doing them a favour, the greatest possible favour indeed; and I am sure I would not take all this trouble were it not that I am convinced it is doing good."

"Oh yes, you are so good-natured, you are always trying to oblige. And what then would you have me to do?"

"Why I would have you call upon Lady Glenmore to-day, and you may tell her how she ought to dress, and to demean herself in public. And when she is in public, you may take care that no one speaks to her but those whom we approve of; and should any of her vulgar relations by any accident affect to get near her, you can contrive to draw her away, and carry her off to some other place. Thus, my dear Lady Ellersby, I think, after having explained this business so far, I need say no more, though I could talk for hours on the subject," Lady Ellersby yawned instinctively; "but the line of conduct I wish you to adopt has been so minutely pointed out, that I think you cannot possibly misunderstand it. And now I will go to Lady Tenderden and the rest, and I flatter myself no *diplomate* ever played his part with more skill. Depend upon it I will continue to do my utmost endeavour to succeed in this affair, which I feel persuaded is of considerable consequence to our society. Not, as I before said, that I would ever, either in great or little matters, stoop to contrivance. I like to persuade people for their good, and would have all the world act with a liberal and free exercise of their own rightful powers; the right of reason which every individual ought to exert and use in his own behalf. Ah, if all governments could but be persuaded of this, and be ruled in their determinations by this noble motive of action, how differently things in general would be managed from what they are! Kings would no longer be puppets of state, but be obliged in self-defence to become rational people, and not to depend on their ministers and favourites; and ministers would not depend on each other as they do, but every body in his own sphere would be doing all he could to tend to the public weal."

Lady Tilney had once again got on her favourite theme; and on these occasions she never found out that the one part of her discourse generally contradicted the other, and that her *meaning* virtually did so where her *words* did not, for it was always herself who was to be the mover and law-giver. But this was all matter of moonshine to her present auditress, who at length shewed unequivocal symptoms of inattention, and even hinted that it was time for her to rise. So at length Lady Tilney, reiterating the part she assigned to her respecting Lady Glenmore, took a tender leave and departed.

Her next visit was made to Lady Tenderden.

"Ah!" she said, on meeting her, after the first greetings, "what a relief it is to have to converse with a rational being, one who understands the meaning of things in general. I have just been talking to poor dear Lady Ellersby, who is, between ourselves, become more than ever thick, and indolent—she actually cannot understand any thing *consecutively*; however, I have, I think, at last put her in a right track upon the subject which I must now discuss with you."

"I know," said Lady Tenderden, interrupting her (for patience was not her *forte*) "what you would say. The Glenmores are arrived, and—"

"Exactly; and it is necessary we talk the matter over, and settle precisely the *marche du jeu.*"

"Oh! by all means, take *la petite Georgina en main, et l'affaire est faite—je m'en charge.*"

"That is precisely what I wished;—nobody is better calculated for that office. In the multiplicity of things which I have to do," said Lady Tilney, "it is not possible that I should pay that sort of attention which she will require, for she is very childish, perfectly ignorant of the ways of the world, almost a simpleton, and our society might be entirely broken up and destroyed, if we allowed her, without proper caution being previously observed, to come in amongst us. At the same time, I think it is of such consequence that we should not altogether lose Lord Glenmore, I mean politically as well as prudentially speaking, that it does appear to me to be quite worth while to take the trouble of forming that little wife of his, and making her one of us."

"Oh, *certainement*," replied Lady Tenderden. "Besides, Lord Glenmore is charming; *il fera fureur*, when he becomes a little more polished, and I shall with infinite pleasure *consacré* some hours to the instruction of *la petite ladi qui seroit à ravir si elle n'avoit pas l'air d'un mouton qui rève.*"

36

"Exactly," cried Lady Tilney, "but that is of no consequence."

"Oh, none in the world," responded Lady Tenderden.

"Well then, my dear, that is finally arranged, and I shall now only have to go to the Glenmores to-morrow; but if it be possible, *you* had better see her to-day, and above all things secure her coming to the Ellersby's party, and Lady Hamlet Vernon's on Sunday, and to our own party on the water on Monday, and to the Opera with you on Tuesday, and so on; in short, taking care only that not one day shall be lost or misapplied."

"Depend upon me; and now then farewell, my dear Lady Tenderden. We meet to-night?"

"Of course. *Soyez toujours séduisante comme à present; cette capotte jaune est délicieuse; elle vous va à ravir.*"

"*Flatteuse,*" rejoined Lady Tilney in a tone of languishing satisfaction, and so they parted mutually pleased. Lady Tenderden, true to her promise, drove straight to Lady Glenmore's, and found her at home. Having expressed her satisfaction at this fortunate circumstance, one too of such rare occurrence, she praised every part of her dress, and inquiring of the Paris fashions, thus proceeded: "And now, my fair queen, you are truly an enviable personage—*you*, if any body ever had, have really *beau jeu*, every thing that can make a woman's life truly desirable; a great establishment, magnificent equipages, jewels, and the consideration which attaches to a *haut grade* in society, a distinguished title, *tout enfin qui peut embellir la vie*; truly, *je vous en félicite, ma belle amie*. But you cannot occupy so enviable a position without exciting the most active envy. Now allow me, as a sincere friend, to put you *au courant* of some things, in respect to the true nature of which you may be deceived. There are a certain set of persons, who will very naturally pay you court, and endeavour to obtain your ear; such as the Duchesse D'Hermanton, the Ladies Proby, and Ladies How, and all that tiresome concourse of old dowagers; but be upon your guard against these, and without giving open offence to any body, be sure that you get rid of them in their very first onset."—Lady Glenmore stared. "*Vous ouvrez des grands yeux, ma chère,* but you will soon learn the use of these cautions. If the people I have named send their names, as they will certainly do or visit you, be a long time before you return the call; they are an old-fashioned set, who pique themselves on politeness, and *veille cour* attentions, and feeling affronted by this neglect on your part, they will not so readily or familiarly accost you in public. When they do (for some of them are vulgarly good-natured enough not to take the hint)—when they do accost you, take care to look as if you did not know who they were, and to answer them by monosyllables, if you answer them at all.

"Above all things, never go to their wearisome *At Homes*; but if they attack you with one of their downright speeches, —sorry not to have had the honour, &c. &c.—hoping you had received a card, &c. &c.—curtsey, and say you were vastly sorry, but you forgot the day, or——no no, say *mistook* it; yes, *mistook* it, that is best, because it is a loop-hole that answers for dinner as well as any other party; yes, a mistake of the day is the best recipe I know, for any invitation which you may chance to hesitate about, and perhaps think it possible you might like to accept, and then having done so, repent of it when the time comes—a mistake in the day sets all right. You are *au desespoir,* and *they* must believe you, or make themselves appear ridiculous; it may indeed cost you a note or two, but that is the worst of it, and then *vous en êtes quitte pour la vie.*"

Lady Glenmore, who had been so astonished hitherto that she could not reply, now found herself called upon to make some answer, as there was a pause on the part of Lady Tenderden.

"You have told me so many things," she said, "my dear Lady Tenderden" (smiling as she spoke), "that I am afraid I shall never remember the half of them, particularly as they are upon subjects which, to tell you the truth, do not interest me much, if at all. One thing you said, however, that was very kind, and kindness is not lost upon me I can assure you, which was the cordial expression with which you wished me joy of my happiness. I should indeed be ungrateful if I did not feel warmly obliged to you; only you omitted in the catalogue of my felicities, that, without which there would be no felicity for me—I mean my being the wife of Lord Glenmore; who, had he not possessed any of the adventitious advantages you enumerated, I should equally have preferred to the whole world."

"Oh! *cela va sans dire*, of course such a young and handsome husband is taken into the account; but, my dear young friend, *vous ne voulez pas vous donner des ridicules*, much less render your husband the laughing-stock of all the world, by setting yourself up with him *en scène de Berger et Bergere*; besides, permit me to say, that is just the way to lose him. If you are always at his elbow, watching him *en furet*, depend upon it he will soon think you are jealous, and following him out of curiosity. Now there is nothing a man can so ill bear as the idea of being watched, particularly by a wife; besides, all his male friends would avoid him if they saw he had such an Argus—for, beautiful as you are, you must not have an hundred eyes, to spy out every thing your husband does; no no, my dear, when you are *en tête-à-tête*, it is all well enough, this new-married fondness; but it will soon evaporate, take my word for it, and then you will be dying to break the troublesome habit *de part et d'autre*, and will not know how to set about it: take great care, *ma chère ladi*, to begin as you mean to go on."

"Certainly," replied Lady Glenmore, "I have but one meaning, one intention—that is, to love and be loved; and I shall never, I hope, do any thing which can run counter to that prime business, that prime duty of my life."

"Oh!" cried Lady Tenderden, perceiving she had gone too far, "it is quite delightful to hear you. You are, I am sure, destined to be a phœnix" (sneeringly); "and proud indeed must any woman be to view one of her own sex so well calculated to be a glory and honour to it. I was only warning you against certain appearances, certain misapprehensions, which persons of your turn of mind are liable to fall into, and which might be the very means of depriving you of that which you are so anxious to retain. I know the world, believe me, my dear young friend, and there is nothing in it I can so ill endure to see, as an assumption of a happiness which is out of the common line. If you enjoy such a superlative felicity, *tant mieux pour vous*, but do not make an *étalage* of it, for either its reality will be questioned, or they will take care it shall not long be one; whereas if you do as other people do, you will be allowed to go on quietly, and you may perhaps carry on this sort of romantic view of life much longer than persons in general do."

Lady Glenmore, who had listened with painful earnestness to this insidious advice, now felt her heart swell, and the tears bursting from her eyes. "And must I really," she said in a voice of suffocation, "pretend to be indifferent to my husband, in order to retain his love?"

"Certainly, my dear child; *peut on être si enfant*" (observing her emotion), "as to allow yourself to be thus moved about such a trifle; take my advice, and you will never lose that sort of hold over his affections which it is so charming, I allow, to

40

possess. Shew him that you can have other men at your feet —that you are not, in short, dependent upon him for any thing *faites vous un sort,* in short, *et vous ne vous en répentirez pas.*"

"And pray, how am I to set about this sort of life?"

"Why nothing so easy; simply, go constantly out, and take care to have one or two young men *de la première volée* always about you; never be reduced to be handed out or into any public place by Lord Glenmore; only now and then *pour faire beau voir,* and to shew that you have *des procédés honnêtes* one to the other—or else *par hasard,* but never as a thing of course. Another point is, you must establish an apartment of your own; for you cannot think between married persons how necessary that is, and what an independence it gives to both. It is so very disagreeable to have the exact moment of our going in and coming out commented upon."

"Dear no, pardon me, not at all. I am always glad when Lord Glenmore says, 'Where have you been so long, Georgina?' because that shews he misses me."

"Oh, of course," said Lady Tenderden, as she always said when she did not know what to say; and inwardly she thought what a world of nature must here be overturned, before any thing artificial can be sown in such a soil! "Well, my dear Lady Glenmore, you come to the Hamlet Vernon's to-morrow night?"

"Yes, I believe so; that is to say, if Lord Glenmore is disengaged."

"Now really we shall all be afraid of such a paragon of love and obedience; or what is worse, we shall all laugh at you if you give *tête baissé* into that sort of ultra propriety. What can Lord Glenmore's engagements have to do with your coming or not coming to Lady Hamlet Vernon's?" Lady Glenmore blushed, and confessed that she did not wish to go out if Lord Glenmore did not.

"Well, my dear, I see the terrible re-action in perspective which must succeed to all this red-hot love; and it is mighty well for the moment; only you are laying up, *croyez moi,* a store of discontent and dissatisfaction for yourself."

At this moment a servant entered, and laid a visiting card on the table. "Oh, Mr. Leslie Winyard," said Lady Tenderden, taking it up, "a vastly agreeable creature: you will let him in of course."

"No," answered Lady Glenmore, "the only thing Lord Glenmore does not wish me to do, as a young married woman, is to receive young men as morning visitors, and I have no wish to disobey him; therefore Mr. Leslie Winyard has been included in the general order I gave to that effect."

"*Je tombe de mon haut;* well, certainly, I never should have guessed that Lord Glenmore, that handsome, young, gay Lothario, would have turned out such a tyrant; and to commence before the honey-moon be well nigh over to shew the cloven-foot of *husbandism,* is really putting a seal to that tyranny with a vengeance! And he—he too, of *all persons,* to pretend—but I believe that is always the way, these men *à bonnes fortunes* do always make the most insufferable husbands."

"I am sure," replied Lady Glenmore, with an air of offended dignity which astonished Lady Tenderden, "I am sure Lord Glenmore desires nothing of me but what he conceives is for my own happiness; and I am perfectly willing to obey him in every thing, far less in such a matter of indifference as this." Her cheeks here grew redder and redder during every word of Lady Tenderden's insidious speech. The melancholy, uneasy expression, nevertheless, which in despite of herself

42

threw a cast of restless inquiry into her countenance, as though she would have asked "to what do you allude?" did not pass unobserved by Lady Tenderden, and she conceived it to be a good time to let the poison work which she had thus insidiously distilled; so she arose to take her leave, and with apparent carelessness said, "*Au reste,* remember," and she spoke in a soothing tone of commiseration, as if she wished, were it possible, to have withdrawn, or at least to soften the words she had uttered, "remember, Lord Glenmore is not a bit worse than other men, they are all alike; and really I think him singularly agreeable, so do not let any thing I have said give you a moment's uneasiness."

She knew the rankling arrow was in Lady Glenmore's heart. "You have nothing to do but to take your own way, and keep it well in mind that all husbands take theirs, and my word for it, if you only follow this counsel, you will live *en Tourtereaux*, and lead a very happy life."

"I have no doubt I shall do that," said Lady Glenmore, half-crying.

"Believe me, *cher enfant,* whenever you feel the least melancholy or uneasy, send for me, and I shall put all to rights for you in a moment; you are a delightful, an unique creature; I really love you, and him too; you know, he was my play-fellow when we were children, therefore I take a particular interest in you both, and am alike the friend of each. Come, dry these beauteous eyes, whose brightness ought not to be dimmed by a tear; come, take a drive with me in the Park." Lady Glenmore hesitated as she replied:

"I expect Lord Glenmore every moment; he promised to drive me in his phaeton. He was to have been here an hour ago" (looking anxiously at the clock).

"Well, then, if he is an hour after his appointment, you would not surely wait for him any longer? Depend upon it he has been engaged by some business, or it may be love of virtù or politics, *que sçai-je*—come let us go and look for him; my life for it we shall meet him in the Park."

"Perhaps so," said the youthful Georgina with a sigh, who evidently assented to Lady Tenderden's proposal for no other reason than that the hope might be realized;—and ordering the servant who answered her bell, to tell her maid to arrange her shawl, she followed her *friend* to her carriage.

When they reached the Park her eyes wandered from one figure to another in quest of Lord Glenmore; in vain—the admiration of the passing throng who courted her attention had no attraction for her, she saw not the only object she wished to see, and returned wearied and dispirited, notwithstanding all Lady Tenderden's endeavours to amuse and dissipate her thoughts. The moment she came home, however, she had the satisfaction of finding her husband already there, and she scarcely waited to say adieu to Lady Tenderden before she flew up stairs to him. After her first greeting, he asked her where and with whom she had been; and on telling him, he said, "I am glad, love, that you like Lady Tenderden, for she has a thousand good qualities;" (*a façon de parler* by the way, which is often taken upon trust from one month to another, and frequently bears no true meaning.) Lord Glenmore continued: "Yes, she has a thousand good qualities, and is very clever and agreeable in her way, and has that perfect *usage du monde* which has so much charm, and which besides may be of real advantage to a young person like yourself entering on the scene; I am quite rejoiced that she is your friend. It is true she sometimes overpasses that line of *retenue* which I might like my young wife to observe; yet she has never been charged with any real fault, and in adopting what is best, you can leave out such parts of her manners and conduct as may not exactly suit your age and taste. In short, I think she is a very useful acquaintance, and you may safely listen to her advice respecting your conduct in the world; but after a little experience, my sweet Georgina, you may make your own choice of intimates, and I am sure that selection will always be well and wisely made."

Lady Glenmore listened attentively to her husband, and sighed as she recalled to mind the nature of the advice which she had already received; but thought, "well, then, Lady Tenderden was right after all, and I must not tell Glenmore. How childish and silly I was in having been so vexed about his not coming home this morning,—still less must I tell him of her cautioning me against pursuing him, for should he know that I had a thought of doing so, it might probably produce the effect she predicted."

With this idea thus unfortunately impressed upon her mind by what her husband had unthinkingly said, Lady Glenmore remained silent. The hour of dressing now called them to their toilette, and the subject was not at that time renewed.

CHAPTER III.

JEALOUSY.

AFTER Lord Albert had parted with his friend in the Park, he returned again to Lady Dunmelraise's house; but still in vain—they came not. The agony of suspense, when prolonged, is perhaps the severest which the human mind can know; but like all chastisements or corrections, it is never sent without a meaning, and if entertained as it is mercifully intended it should be, we shall reap the fruits of the trial.

In the present case, Lord Albert's disappointment brought back a livelier sense of the attachment he really felt for Lady Adeline, and awoke all those tender fears and reminiscences which cherish love, but which a too great security of possession had for the present blunted, or at least laid in abeyance. He now wondered how he could have suffered so much time to elapse without writing to her. He wondered, too, that he had not heard from her; she had not then missed the blank in his part of the correspondence; and it was evident some other interest had supplied that one in her heart.—He looked at her picture, as if he could read in that image an answer to these various surmises; but it was placid, and serene—it smiled as was her wont, and he felt displeased at the senseless portrait, for an expression which he could not have borne her to wear, had she really known what his fears and feelings were. He shut the case and pushed it from him;—he felt angry—and then ashamed—for conscience goaded him with its sting, and in turn questioned him, as to his right of indulging one such sensation against *her*, whom in fact he knew he had neglected: but all this process of mental analization was salutary, and as he came by degrees to know himself better, he was enabled to form a truer estimation, not only of the amiable person to whom he was bound by every tie of honour, but of the true nature of real worth.

At length, on the fourth morning from that on which he met Lord Glenmore, he found in North Audley Street a note from Lady Adeline. "A note only!" he said, hastily breaking the seal. It was written from an inn on the road; it informed him that Lady Dunmelraise had borne the journey very ill, which had occasioned them to stop frequently; but that they would reach town she hoped on the following evening. Lord Albert turned quickly to the date, and found that it was of the preceding day, so that he might expect their arrival that very evening. A gleam of delightful anticipation now shed joy over his heart. We easily gloss over our own faults; and Lord Albert found all his self-reproaches for neglect and temporary coldness merged in the fondness he actually felt at that moment, and his present determination to abide by, and act upon this feeling, silenced all self-accusation. With a beating pulse, and an emotion he did not wish to quell, he determined on not leaving the house till he should once more have seen *his* Adeline.

He seated himself, therefore, in the drawing-room, and gave a loose to those pleasurable sensations which now flowed in upon him. The apartment had been prepared for Lady Dunmelraise, and all the usual objects in her own and her daughter's occupations were set in their wonted places. He recognized with transport a thousand trifling circumstances connected with them, which brought his love, his *own* love, more vividly before his eyes. As he carefully enumerated and dwelt upon these, his eyes rested on a vacant space in the wall near the piano-forte, where a drawing of himself had hung; and the enchanting thought that it had been her companion in the country, came in aid of all the rest to soften and gladden every sensation of his heart. As his eyes wandered over the apartment in quest of fresh food for delight, they rested on a parcel of papers, and letters, lying on the writing table. He turned them over, hardly knowing why he did so, when a frank from Restormel, directed to Lady Adeline Seymour, gave him an unpleasant shock, and he dropped it with a sudden revulsion of sensation that was any thing but gentle.

He again resumed the letter, turned it round and round, looked at the seal—it was a coat of arms, but the motto, *"for life,"* was a peculiar one. He wondered to what family it belonged; he thought of consulting some heraldic work in order to discover, when the sound of a heavy laden carriage passing in the street, drew off his attention. He flew to the window—it was a family coach, but one glance told him it was not that of Lady Dunmelraise. Back he came to the letter table; again *the letter* was before his eyes—*the letter*, for amongst many he saw but one.

"It is surprising," he said to himself, "that Adeline should have a correspondent at Restormel, and I not know of it; but shortly, very shortly, this mystery shall be solved. I will ask her at once—but carelessly, naturally, who is her unknown friend at Restormel? Ask her? no, she will of course tell me, if she has formed any new acquaintance with whom she is sufficiently intimate to correspond, and if she does not of herself tell me, I shall never *inquire* into the matter—indeed why should I? No, there is nothing renders a man so silly as jealousy, or throws him so much in a woman's power as letting her see he is jealous."

With these, and many such contradictory reasonings as

48

these, did Lord Albert continue to pace the room along and across, and every now and then stop and fix his eyes on the offending letter; when again a sound attracted him to the window, and though it was dusk, and objects were indistinctly seen at a distance, he recognized the well-known equipage. The next moment he was in the street; and the next it drove up to the door. He heard Lady Adeline's soft voice cry out, "There's Albert!" as she half turned to her mother, and kept kissing her hand to himself. The carriage door was opened, and she sprang out, receiving the pressure of his hand with an answering expression of fondness.

"Dear Albert, how do you do? have you not thought we were an age on the road? But I hope you received my note." Ere he could reply, Lady Dunmelraise's extended hand was cordially presented to him, and as affectionately taken; and while each rested on his arm on entering the house, he felt in the kindly pressure of both that he was as welcome to them as ever.

When he had assisted Lady Dunmelraise, who moved feebly, to the drawing-room, and placed her pillows on the couch, even in this moment of joyous re-union, he could not fail to observe what ravages sickness had made in her frame since they last met; and as he expressed, though in modified terms, in order not to alarm her, the regret he felt at seeing her so unwell, he observed the eyes of Lady Adeline fixed upon him, in order to read his real opinion on the first sight he had of her mother; and before he could regulate his own feelings on the subject, those of Lady Adeline's overshadowed her countenance with an expression of sadness she was not prepared to command, while the tears rushed to her eyes. Again holding out her hand to Lord Albert, while a smile of mingled joy and sorrow beamed over her features, and partly dispersed the cloud, she said,

"All will be well *now*; my dearest mamma will soon be better

—joy and happiness will once again be our's." Lord Albert thanked her with his eloquent eyes; and as he impressed a kiss on her offered hand, he replied:

"How fortunate that I received your letter when I did, for in another hour I should have been on my way to Dunmelraise."

"Indeed!" said Lady Adeline, her eyes sparkling with pleasure.

"Yes; and I had, but for something which detained me, been on my road there long before your letter arrived."

"That would indeed have been unfortunate," said Lady Dunmelraise; "to have missed you after so long hoping to have seen you there in vain, would have doubled our regret;" she spoke with a tone of something like reproach, at least so Lord Albert took it; and she added, with a melancholy smile, "It is a bad omen that a letter from *Adeline* should have *prevented* you from coming to us."

Lord Albert felt embarrassed; there was something relative to the delay of his coming which he knew he could not explain, and this consciousness made him feel as if he were acting a double part. At this moment Lady Adeline perceived the letters lying on the table, and taking them up, she glanced her eye over them as she turned them round one by one, saying, "this is for you, mamma—and this—and this—and this, as she handed them to Lady Dunmelraise—but this one is for myself." Lord Albert's attention had from the first moment of her taking up the letters been riveted upon her, and now with ill-concealed anxiety he watched every turn of her countenance, while she broke the seal and perused the letter. She read it, he conceived, with great interest; and said, when she had concluded, addressing Lady Dunmelraise—

"It is a kind word of inquiry for you, my dear mamma, from

50

George Foley." Lord Albert changed colour as this name was pronounced; but neither she nor Lady Dunmelraise observed the circumstance, and this gave him leisure and power to recover from the confusion he experienced. Lady Adeline again resumed, after a short pause, "You must have met Mr. Foley at Restormel, Albert; what do you think of him?"

"I had little opportunity of judging of him," replied Lord Albert, hesitating as he spoke; "but he was only at Restormel for a part of the time I was there. He had, however, a strong recommendation to my favourable opinion, from the warm terms of praise and admiration in which he mentioned you, Adeline." She smiled, and without any alteration of manner went on to say:

"I am afraid then he has *too* favourable an opinion of me; and if he has raised your expectations so high of my improvement since last we met, I shall have reason to lament your having become acquainted with him; but he is such an *adorateur* of mamma's, that he thinks every thing that belongs to her is perfection!"

Notwithstanding Lady Adeline's seeming calmness while speaking of Mr. Foley—notwithstanding the natural and ingenuous expression of her words and countenance, Lord Albert could not divest himself of the idea that Mr. Foley had some undue power over her affections. It is easy, perhaps, to shut the door against evil thoughts; but when once they are admitted, they obtain a footing and a consequence which it was never intended that they should have. Beware, all ye who love, of admitting one spark of jealousy into your breasts, without immediately quenching the same by open and free discussion with the object of your affections! But there lies the difficulty—we are ashamed of harbouring an injurious thought of those we love; or rather, we are ashamed of *confessing* that we do so; and we go on in the danger of concealment, rather than by humbling our pride, and laying open our error, obtain the probable chance of having it exposed, and removed. While monosyllables of indifferent import dropped from Lord Albert's lips, he was in his heart cherishing the false notion that had the letter, which gave him so much uneasiness, been entirely of the import which Lady Adeline represented it to be, it would have been more natural to have addressed it to Lady Dunmelraise herself.

He did not, indeed, dare to impugn Lady Adeline's truth: but he conceived that no other man should presume to have an interest in her—in her who *belonged to himself* (every man will understand this), which could entitle him to hold a correspondence with her. He consequently became abstracted, and there was a sort of restraint upon the ease of his manner and conversation, of which Lady Dunmelraise's penetration soon made her aware, and to which even the young and unsuspecting Adeline could not remain wholly blind.

In order to replace things on the footing which they had been formerly, and which on their first meeting they still appeared to be, Lady Adeline turned the discourse to her pursuits in the country, and spoke in detail of her drawing, her music, her flower-garden, and the families of the poor in their neighbourhood whom she and Lord Albert had so often visited together.

"You remember," she said, "poor Betsy Colville, who never recovered the loss of her lover who was shipwrecked; she is still in the same state. She goes every day to the gate where they last parted, takes out the broken sixpence he gave her at their last interview; and having returned home, looks in her father's face, and says '*to-morrow*.' She never repines, never misses church—joins in family worship; but her poor mind is touched, and she can no longer do the work of the house or tend on her aged parents. I have therefore paid my chief attentions to that family—and they are so grateful—so grateful, too, for what you have done for them. The myrtle we planted together, Albert, on the gable-end of the house, now nearly reaches the thatch; and in all their distress about their daughter, the good old pair have never forgotten to tend that plant. Mr. Foley and I rode or walked there every day."

The latter words of this discourse poisoned all the sweetness of the preceding part; and the idea of Mr. Foley became associated in Lord Albert's distempered mind, with all the interest and all the enthusiasm expressed by Lady Adeline; so that he read in her descriptions of her mode of having passed her time, and the pleasure she had innocently enjoyed, nothing but her love of Mr. Foley's company.

Lord Albert became still more silent, or spoke only in broken sentences; and a deeper gloom gradually spread over each of the three individuals, usurping the place of that cordial outpouring of the heart, which had at first rendered the moment of meeting so delightful. After a silence, during which Lady Adeline and Lady Dunmelraise appeared mutually affected by the awkwardness which the change in Lord Albert's manner had excited, yet anxious to conceal from each other the knowledge that such was the case—they felt relieved, when he took up a newspaper, and read aloud the announcement of an approaching drawing-room.

Lady Dunmelraise, glad of an opportunity to find some subject of discourse foreign to the thoughts which obtruded themselves so painfully upon her, said, "Well, Adeline, that is a favourable circumstance, *à quelque chose malheur est bon;* had I not been so much worse exactly at this very time, we had perhaps not been in London; for though I have for some months past wished you to be presented at court, we might, ten to one, not have had courage to leave

Dunmelraise at this sweet season; but as it is, the opportunity must not be lost, and the only question is, by whom shall the presentation take place—for alas! I am not able myself to have that pleasure, and I fear my dear sister Lady Delamere will not either;" then pausing a moment, she added, "perhaps, Lord Albert, Lady Tresyllian will kindly take that office, if she is to be in town."

"I am sure she would readily comply with any wish of yours; but I know my mother has, in a great measure, given up the London world, and has not been at any of the drawing-rooms during the present reign; but, perhaps, on such an occasion, she might be induced to forego her determination of retreat."

"Oh, I would not for the world," said Lady Adeline, "torment Lady Tresyllian about it; for," she added, smiling, "you know how very little I care about such things."

"It is well," said Lady Dunmelraise, "to hold every thing in estimation according to its due value. Most young persons are *too* fond of the gaieties and pleasures of the world; but you, my dear Adeline, perhaps contemn them in one sweeping clause of indifference, without having properly considered to what advantages they may tend when resorted to in due degree, and in subordination to better pursuits. A drawing-room I hold to be one of those very few worldly pageants which are connected with some valuable and estimable feelings; the attending them is an homage due to the state of the sovereign; they uphold the aristocracy of the country, which is one of the three great powers of government, now too much, too dangerously set aside; and they ought to, and do in great measure, keep up those barriers in society, which prevent an indiscriminate admission of vice and virtue, at least as far as regards an outward respect to the *appearances of decorum*. Whenever drawing-rooms shall be abolished, you will see that much

54

greater licence in society will take place. The countenance of the sovereign, the right to be in his presence, is one which none would voluntarily resign; and to avoid losing it, is a check upon the conduct of many, who are not regulated by better motives; while those who are, will always duly appreciate those honours which flow from monarchs, and which form a part of our glorious constitution. 'Love God, honour the king,' is the good old adage; and with this conviction on my mind, and the remembrance of that loyalty and attachment to the present House of Hanover which your ancestors have ever displayed, even to the sacrifice of their lives and fortunes, my Adeline, I have set my heart on your being presented to your king; and the only consideration is, who shall be the person to present you."

"Well, dearest mamma," replied Lady Adeline, "any thing you wish, I shall be delighted to do, and I make no doubt you are perfectly right; only I did not feel the least anxious, and I wished to set your mind at rest upon the subject of my going into public." Lord Albert said, with an expression of melancholy and displeasure, "It is quite unnatural for a young person of your age, Adeline, to affect to despise the amusements of the world; and unless you have some *cause* for doing so, best known to yourself, I confess I do not understand it."

Lady Adeline was too quick-sighted not to perceive that something or other pained and displeased Lord Albert, and had they been quite alone, she might have asked him the occasion of this change in his humour; but as it was, she did not dare to question him; and by way of turning the conversation into another channel, she inquired, of whom consisted the party at Restormel; if they were clever, or distinguished, or agreeable; and whether the mode of life there was to his taste? Lord Albert seemed to awake out of a sort of reverie into which he had fallen, and his countenance was agitated by many commingling expressions as he replied,

"I really can hardly tell you; there were the Tilneys, the Tenderdens, the Boileaus, Lady Hamlet Vernon, Mr. Leslie Winyard. At that sort of party there is little occasion for the display of talent, and people are glad to be quiet for a few days when they go to their country houses; so that each individual is thinking more of repose than of shining. As to their mode of life, it was pretty nearly, I think, what it is when they are in town."

Though Lord Albert spoke this in a hurried tone, he felt as though he had got well over a difficulty. But the remark Lady Dunmelraise made upon his answer, did not particularly serve his turn at the moment:—"Either the persons who I heard composed that party, or Lord Albert, must be much changed since I knew them, if they could be in unison," and she fixed her eyes upon him;—his embarrassment was visible, and did not subside as she went on to speak particularly of Lady Hamlet Vernon: "She remembered her marriage," she said, and commented upon those sort of marriages, saying, "that all intriguing schemes were detestable, but those respecting marriage were of all others the most thoroughly wicked and despicable. Lady Hamlet's conduct, too, after marriage was not very praiseworthy: if a woman sacrifice every other consideration in allying herself to her husband for the sake of aggrandizement, she must at least continue to act upon that system, and if possible wash out the disgrace of such an act (for I consider it to be no less) by her subsequent mode of behaviour, and the dignified uses to which she applies her power. But in the present instance this was far from being the case, and she had allowed an apparent levity of conduct, at least, to sully her character. In one instance, I *know*, she has drawn a person, in whom I feel great interest, into a manner of life, and an idleness of existence, which, to call it by no harsher name, is one of vanity and folly; but I had hoped her influence was over in that quarter."

"As I do not know to what you allude," rejoined Lord Albert, "I cannot exactly reply; but certainly Lady Hamlet Vernon is very handsome, very agreeable, and, for aught I know to the contrary, leads now a very good sort of life. She has a finely-disposed heart, and, I should think, is better than half the people who find fault with her. If, from having married an old *roué*, she was thrown into danger, which her personal charms rendered very likely to have been the case, kindness I am sure would at any time open her eyes to avoid these; whereas undue severity might make her rush headlong into them—for harsh opinions in similar cases, nine times out of ten, drive such persons from bad to worse."

"I conceive," said Lady Dunmelraise, "that this may sometimes be the case; but it is frequently only an excuse for not choosing to hear the truth told. However, there is a society, of which Lady Hamlet Vernon is one, which I hold to be the subverter of every thing estimable. Its great danger is the specious ease and indifference of those who compose it, the system being without any system whatever. The great gentleness of manner and entire freedom, which seem to be its characteristics, are its most dangerous snares. No consecutive speech upon any subject, no power of reasoning, no appeal to religion, are tolerated by these persons. They have a lawless form of self-government indeed, by which they keep up their own sect and set,—but there is a mystery in the delusions which they cast around their victims, the more difficult to detect since the whole of their lives is spent in a seeming carelessness about every thing.

57

"The warning voice of a parent can alone put a young and unsuspecting member of society on his guard against being drawn into this vortex; but it is the young married persons to whom such warning is more particularly necessary. However, because there are persons, who by artful intrigue arrogate to themselves a certain consideration, which they receive from the uninstructed and unwary, and whose ways are certainly not those of pleasantness or peace—we are not to say but that there are others who to the highest rank unite the highest principles, and who reflect honour on the class to which they belong—persons who consider their high stations as being the gifts of God, and themselves as responsible agents. Yes, the true nobility of Britain will yield to none other of any country for intrinsic worth; all the virtues adorn their families, and religion and honour stamp them with that true nobility of soul, without which all distinction is but a beacon of disgrace.

"It is not, therefore, because a few worthless or foolish persons, in the vast concourse of London society, affect an exclusiveness which rests on no basis of real worth or dignity, but on the very reverse, that all intercourse with the world is to be avoided, or all innocent pleasure to be denied to young persons; and I should be exceedingly disappointed to see my Adeline retiring from her state and station, and coming to have a distaste for its amusements, because I feel certain that so violent a re-action is not natural, and that the real way to be of service to herself and others, is to fulfil the rank and station of life wherein she is placed, and in fact to do as our great inimitable Pattern did —to go about doing good."

Lord Albert's feelings, while Lady Dunmelraise was speaking, had undergone many changes, but the last was that of pleasurable approval at finding Lady Dunmelraise's opinion so much in coincidence with his own—and he said, in his own natural warm manner, "I hope Adeline will feel quite convinced, by your sensible manner, my dear Lady Dunmelraise, of representing this matter, that there is no virtue, nothing commendable indeed, in despising or condemning the world *en masse*, and that there is just as much real good to be done by living in as living out of it. True virtue does not lie in time or place—it is of all times, of all places; and it is a narrow, bigoted view of the subject alone, which partakes of monastic rigour and hypocritical ambition under the garb of humility, which would promulgate any other doctrine."

"My dear Albert, you know that I have no wish but to please mamma and you; and I need not pretend but that I shall be exceedingly diverted by going to public places. All I meant to say was, not to make yourselves uneasy about finding a *chaperon* for me, because I am perfectly contented to remain as I am—although I might be equally well diverted in leading what is called a gayer life."

Lord Albert's countenance relapsed into brightness as he said, taking her hand and putting it to his lips, "You are a dear and a rare creature—is she not, Lady Dunmelraise?"—and this appeal Lady Dunmelraise felt no inclination to controvert; but, rejoicing in the present disposition which she once more beheld in her future son-in-law, she now dismissed him for the evening, saying, "Adeline and I require some repose, that we may be fresh to-morrow for all the great events to which we shall look forward with pleasure, I am sure, as you seem to be quite of our way of thinking respecting her *début* in the great world—and so good night." The wish was reiterated kindly, warmly, by all parties, and they parted happier even than they had met.

As soon as Lord Albert reached his hotel, he found a note from Lady Hamlet Vernon, announcing her arrival from Restormel, and requesting to see him. In an instant, as though by magic, his doubts and fears respecting Lady Adeline returned; for with Lady Hamlet Vernon was connected the recollection of her mysterious note at Restormel, on the morning of his departure from thence—and with that recollection George Foley was but too deeply mingled. Then ensued a chaos in his mind, one thought chasing another, and none abiding to fix any purpose or decide any measure. At one moment he determined—if such passing impulse can be called determination—not to go near Lady Hamlet; but the next he thought she had shewn so much true interest for him—she had listened so often to his rebukes—apparently with more pleasure than she did to praise from others—that he should be ungrateful to avoid her *now*, because other dearer interests filled up his time and his heart, and he finally resolved on obeying her wishes, and visiting her the next day.

In the morning of that day, before he had finished his late breakfast, and ere he was prepared to deny himself, the door of his apartment opened, and Mr. Foley was close to him ere his servant had time to announce his name.

"I am come," said the latter, with his polite and honeyed phrase, "to bring you pleasant tidings, which I trust will apologize for this my early intrusion. I am just arrived from South Audley Street, where I had the happiness of finding our friends pretty well; Lady Dunmelraise, indeed, was not up, having been fatigued by her journey; but Lady Adeline is blooming in beauty—I do not know when I have seen her looking better." Lord Albert bowed, and in his coldest manner replied, "he was very happy indeed to hear that Lady Adeline Seymour was so well, and he hoped, when he should make his personal inquiries, to find Lady Dunmelraise in the drawing-room."

Mr. Foley was too penetrating not to see that this information, as it came from him, conveyed no pleasurable feeling; but affecting not to observe this, he went on to talk of the late party at Restormel—spoke of Lady Hamlet Vernon as being a delightful creature, and drew a kind of parallel *raisonné* between her character and that of Lady Adeline's. Lord Albert was thinking, all the time he spoke, of the impertinent assumption of Mr. Foley's addressing him on the subject of Lady Adeline, and discussing her merits, as though he were not aware of them, and had not a better right and ampler means to know and to value them.

Still there was a suavity—a delicacy even, in Mr. Foley's mode of expressing himself, which gave no tangible opportunity to shew offence; and Lord Albert, though writhing under impatience, was obliged to control himself. As soon as he could possibly contrive to do so, he changed the conversation, and spoke of the Opera, the Exhibition, the topics of the day—of all, in short, that was most uninteresting to him; and carried on an under current of thought all the time on the impropriety Adeline had been guilty of, in receiving Mr. Foley without her mother's presence to sanction such a visit, and on going himself directly to South Audley Street, in order that he might disclose to her his opinion on the inexpediency of such a measure, as that of her receiving the visits of young men when alone. But though the evident abstraction of Lord Albert D'Esterre rather increased than diminished, still Mr. Foley sat on, and sometimes rose to make a remark on a picture—sometimes opened a book, and commented upon its contents. Similar provocation must have occurred to every one at some time or other, and it is in vain to describe what, after all, no description can do justice to. A note arrived for Lord Albert—it was from Lady Adeline—very kind, but desiring him not to come to South Audley Street till four o'clock—saying she was going, by her mamma's desire, to see her aunt Lady Delamere, who was confined by a feverish cold, and could not leave her chamber to come to them.

Lord Albert's mortification was painted on his countenance. "If you have nothing better to do this morning, D'Esterre, and that your note does not otherwise take up your time, will you accompany me to Lady Hamlet Vernon's?" Lord Albert felt, "what, am I to be balked, dogged, forestalled in every trifling circumstance by this man!" but he *said*, hesitating as he spoke, "yes—no, that is to say, I had an engagement, but it is postponed for the present—therefore, if you please, I will accompany you to Lady Hamlet's door;" and Mr. Foley, evidently triumphing in having foiled Lord Albert's real intentions, whatever they might be, but maintaining still his quiet composure, offered Lord Albert his arm, and they walked together towards Grosvenor Square, each talking of one thing and thinking of another.

CHAPTER IV.

AN EXCLUSIVE MORNING PARTY.

As they walked along between Lord Albert's house and that of their destination, one idea took the lead in D'Esterre's mind—it was the hope of obtaining from Lady Hamlet Vernon an elucidation of the mysterious expressions contained in her note. He formed a thousand plans how he should contrive to remain alone with her, after Mr. Foley should take his leave, for he made no question but that he would be the first to end his visit; and he settled it in his own mind that he would affect to have some message to give Lady Hamlet, which might afford him an opportunity of procuring the interview he so eagerly desired: but almost always, in similar circumstances, none of these minor events occur as we intend they should; and the first object Lord Albert saw on entering Lady Hamlet Vernon's drawing-room was Lady Tenderden, sitting at a writing table, having taken off her bonnet as though she had come upon some particular occasion, and was fixed there for a considerable time.

"Ah! Lord Albert," said Lady Hamlet Vernon, "and Mr. Foley too! Most welcome both.—Restormel was quite dull without you; and besides the comfort one always feels at coming back to the dear dirty streets, after having been banished from them a few days, I am really charmed to find myself once more surrounded by all my friends. Do tell us the news, and sit down—you shall not positively pay me a flying visit—though you, Lord Albert, flew away in such a hurry from Restormel, that we had not time, no not even to say 'farewell;'"—(and she looked at him very significantly as she spoke.) "So before I shall have time now to speak to you, you will be gone again—but if so, it is not *my* fault."

Lord Albert thought that he read the meaning of this speech, and his impatience and anxiety were increased in proportion. It was with the utmost difficulty he could bring himself to leave her side in order to go to the other end of the room, in obedience to Lady Tenderden, who called him every now and then to ask some silly question or other, which he hardly answered; and which induced her, therefore, to beg him to come and sit near her, that she might talk to him comfortably while she was writing: two things which she declared she could do quite well at the same time. As soon as Lady Tenderden had managed this contrivance, Mr. Foley entered into (apparently) a very interesting conversation with Lady Hamlet Vernon; and Lord Albert sat on thorns as his eyes were rivetted on them, while he contrived to answer Lady Tenderden, although it were as if he was playing at cross purposes. Any change was a relief, and the announcement of Lord Glenmore was a real pleasure to him, for he thought his arrival must at least break up the *tête-à-tête* between Lady Hamlet and Mr. Foley, which seemed to him as if it never would end.

After having paid his compliments to Lady Hamlet Vernon and Lady Tenderden, Lord Glenmore accosted his friend, and cordially wished him joy in a sort of half whisper, on Lady Dunmelraise's arrival. But, in Lord Albert's present frame of mind, this congratulation was not received with that open warmth which Lord Glenmore expected; and he dropped the subject, taking up those of the common-place occurrences of the day. The drawing-room was discussed; it was to be fuller than any preceding one. Lady Tilney had declared she would not go—so had Lady Ellersby; "but, nevertheless," said Lord Glenmore, with one of his good-humoured smiles, "I dare say those ladies will not have the cruelty to allow their absence to be regretted when the time arrives; do you think they will, Lady Hamlet Vernon?"

"Most indubitably not, and I make no doubt the *plumassiers* and jewellers are all at this moment in requisition in Lady Tilney's boudoir. But, by the way, Lord Glenmore, your fair lady will of course be presented on your marriage—who is to have the pleasure of presenting her?"

"Who? why of course her mother, Lady Melcomb."

Lady Hamlet Vernon and Lady Tenderden here exchanged the most significant glances, and a silence ensued; which was first broken by Lord Glenmore, who endeavoured to draw Lord Albert into conversation by touching alternately on politics, literature, and all the subjects which he knew were interesting to him; but to which he could only obtain some short answer, that did not promote the flow of the conversation. He began to ask himself whether he could have given Lord Albert any offence, or whether he retained any on account of their interview in the Park; but it was so unlike Lord Albert to take offence where it never was intended to be given, that he concluded (as was in fact the case) that something painful was on his mind, of which he could not divest himself. Having vainly attempted, by raillery as well as by engaging his attention, to get the better of this abstraction and gloom, Lord Glenmore let the matter pass, and addressed his conversation elsewhere; but Lady Tenderden was not to be diverted from her purpose, and she took up the thread of discourse, requesting to know if Lady Adeline Seymour had imposed a vow of silence upon him, or what other cause had so changed him since he was last at Restormel? He pleaded total ignorance of being changed; but the consciousness that he was so, rendered his efforts at disguise only more visible.

Lord Albert rose and sat down; a hundred times he looked at a French clock on the chimney-piece, which of course did not go; and at last requested Mr. Foley to tell him the hour, as he had an engagement which demanded his attention. Having found that it was a full half hour past the time appointed by Lady Adeline, he made his bow to Lady Hamlet Vernon, and was about to leave the room, when she called him back, and said, "of course we all meet in the evening at Lady Tilney's?" There was a glance and an emphasis which accompanied these words, which he could not fail to interpret as an assignation, and one that he determined on his part to keep.

Could Lord Albert have known what was passing in Lady Adeline's mind, while he was thus misspending his time in a false anxiety about a few mysterious words, written, it might be, with no good intent, and indeed it might be without any foundation, he would have hastened away from this idle and unworthy mode of passing his time long before he did; but experience unfortunately must be bought, and although we look upon the actions of others, and comment upon them, it may be with the calm wisdom of unmoved breasts, yet in our own time of trial we are too apt to prove that theory is not practice. One would imagine that it was the easiest thing possible to place one's-self ideally in the situation of another, to feel as he felt, and yet act diametrically opposite to the way in which he acted, in certain circumstances and positions; but this apparent facility of transmigration into the identity of another's being is mere delusion. It may be questioned if any human creature really understands another, and how much less likely is it that he should argue justly on his neighbour's affairs! Oh, if we were more merciful to others, and more severe on ourselves; more humble as to our own merits and more alive to those of our fellow creatures; we should be nearer the mark of justice than we usually are.

While Lord Albert, under the influence of a tormenting incipient jealousy, wasted the hour at Lady Hamlet Vernon's which he should have passed in South Audley Street, Lady Adeline had been with her aunt, Lady Delamere, who, in a true spirit of affectionate solicitude, had nevertheless opened up a source of anxiety and doubt in the breast of her niece, which proved the cause of infinite distress to her. Lady Delamere, after receiving her with all that glow of partial fondness peculiarly characteristic of her family, it might be too much so towards each other, naturally spoke of Lord Albert D'Esterre.

"Ah, my dear Adeline, now the time approaches when, according to your father's will, your final decision respecting the fulfilment of your marriage must take place, my anxious fondness suggests a thousand fears, at least doubts, for your happiness. I beseech you let these four intervening months at least be given, not only to a serious examination of your own heart, but to a clear and vigorous elucidation of the disposition and principles of Lord Albert."

"As to my own heart," replied Lady Adeline with quickness, "it has long not been in my own keeping, for most fortunately, where my duty was directed to place it, there my choice seconded, nay, almost preceded the arrangement. But why should you doubt that, such being the case, my happiness should be endangered? say rather, dearest aunt, confirmed."

"It may be so—I trust it will be so, my sweet Adeline, since your love is fixed; but remember how very serious a step marriage is; and before you are bound for life in the holiest of all ties, again I conjure you to lay aside, inasmuch as you can do so, all the blandishments of love, and consider how

67

far the tastes, the pursuits, the temper, above all the religious tenets of your husband, will be in accordance with your own. Indeed, indeed, people do not reflect seriously *enough* on these points. I ask not any long consideration, any great trial of time or absence—they are both circumstances which may deceive either way; for things viewed at a distance, are not seen in their true light; and one may be as much deceived at the end of a year, as at the end of a month—and life is short. The life of life, the bloom of youth, should not be needlessly withered in pining anxiety. What I ask of you is, during the time you are now to be in town, to go out with moderation into the great world, to see what it has to offer, and to know whether any other person might supersede Lord Albert in your affections; this is as yet a fair and honourable trial. You are *not bound* to each other, if either wishes to break the tie." (Lady Adeline sighed heavily.) "And should you, while together, discover any flaw or imperfection which might make you wish to dissolve the engagement, now is the time; but after marriage, I need not say, my Adeline, that one glance of preference for another is guilt—one wish, foreign to your allegiance as a wife, is *misery*."

There was a pause in the conversation. Lady Adeline felt sorrowful—she scarcely knew why, except indeed it had never occurred to her that any thing could step in to break off her engagement with Lord Albert; and the bare possibility of such an event seemed to unhinge her whole being.

The fact is, Lady Delamere had heard surmises of Lord Albert's intimacy with Lady Hamlet Vernon, and without informing her niece of a report which, after all, might not have any foundation, she yet conceived it to be a duty to put her on her guard, and make her ready to observe any alteration that might have taken place in Lord Albert. She would have told Lady Dunmelraise all that she had heard without disguise; but at present her state of health was such, that she could not think of endangering her life by giving her such information; for she well knew her sister's heart was set upon the match, and that she had long loved Lord Albert as though he had been her son. However, she determined, the moment Lady Dunmelraise was better, to have no concealment from her. It had not been without much self-debate that she had brought herself even to hint any thing like a doubt to Lady Adeline of Lord Albert's truth; and even now, she only endeavoured to prepare her to open her eyes to the conviction, should such a melancholy change have taken place, but without naming the real cause she had for giving her such caution.

As it was, it was quite enough to sadden Lady Adeline; and her air was so dejected when she returned home to Lady Dunmelraise, that the latter feared something had occurred to vex her. "Is my sister worse, dearest child?—I pray you do not conceal the truth from me."

"Oh no;—be not alarmed," she replied, "my aunt hopes, in a day or two, to be able to come to see you, dearest mamma. It is not that—but I have a bad head-ache, and have undergone too much excitement." The look of anxious inquiry which Lady Dunmelraise could not conceal, lessened not Lady Adeline's unhappiness; and as the time which she had appointed for Lord Albert's visit was now far passed, the whole weight of the sad warnings she had received, seemed doubled. At length the peculiar knock—the quick footstep on the stair, told her he was come, and she passed from her mother's bedroom into the adjoining drawing-room to meet him.

They seemed mutually affected by some secret cause; for there was not that cordial clasping of hands—that beaming of eyes—that joyful tone of greeting, which might have been expected to mark their meeting on this occasion: their hands touched coldly—and Lord Albert made no effort to retain her's.

"You have been very much later than I expected, Albert."

"Yes: I could not exactly obey the hour named in your note, as you went out before I could possibly come here this morning; and as you put me off, I had another engagement, which in my turn detained me; however, I was happy to hear you were well from Mr. Foley, who had the pleasure of seeing you, I believe, very early."

"Yes: Mr. Foley, you know, as mamma's *protégé* and *enfant de famille*, has the *entrée* at all hours, and I was drawing when he came in; I thought it was you, and—

"Oh, dear Lady Adeline, you cannot suppose I should take the liberty of inquiring what you were doing—I hope Lady Dunmelraise is better to-day?"

Lady Adeline, under any other influence than that which now influenced her, would have said, "Albert, what is the matter with you? are you displeased?" But her aunt's advice was, "look well to the real state of Lord Albert's affections, and do not allow your own to give a colouring to his, which may not be the true one, were his heart unbiassed by the flattering predilection you so openly profess for him." This advice sealed her lips; and, checking the natural impulse of her heart, she replied to his inquiries about her mother more at length than she would have done, in order to recover a composure she was far from feeling; she allowed all further discussion of her mode of passing the morning to drop.

Lord Albert's restrained, unnatural manner increased, and they both felt relieved when Lady Dunmelraise called from her apartment to her daughter—who obeyed the summons; but returning after a minute's absence, she said,

"Mamma hopes you will dine with us to-day."

"Oh, certainly, if Lady Dunmelraise wishes me to do so:" and as Lady Adeline made no reply, but returned to her mother, Lord Albert departed to dress.

When they met at dinner, Lady Dunmelraise's presence for a time prevented the awkwardness they mutually felt; but she soon found that the conversation was entirely left to her, and could not be long without perceiving that something had occurred which altered Lord Albert's manner. Hoping it, however, only to be one of those fallings-out of lovers which are the renewal of love, Lady Dunmelraise turned the conversation entirely upon the coming drawing-room, and the more interest she seemed to take in her daughter's going into the gay world, the more grave did Lord Albert become: this was a contradiction to what he had expressed respecting that measure, and, as Lady Dunmelraise thought, a caprice of temper, which she was sorry to observe in him. She hoped, however, that the thoughts which involuntarily arose in her mind were groundless, and she determined not to act precipitately; but felt glad that she was come to town, where she would have an opportunity of judging further, and of seeing how matters stood from her own personal observation of Lord Albert's conduct. She considered that to probe her daughter's feelings upon the subject, would be to excite them so painfully, that they might destroy the power of a cool judgment. She therefore resolved to postpone any avowal of her own sentiments, any positive declaration of her own doubts, till the time, which was now fast approaching, for Lady Adeline's ultimate decision, should afford her a proper opportunity of speaking her mind unreservedly to Lord Albert; unless, indeed, circumstances of an imperious kind relative to his conduct should make such a step necessary before that period.

In this disposition of mind, the parties could not enjoy each other's society. The conversation was broken, interrupted, and in itself devoid of interest; so that when Lord Albert arose to take his leave about ten o'clock, Lady Adeline almost felt it a relief. "What, are you going to leave us so soon?" said Lady Dunmelraise, with visible surprise.

"I am sorry that a particular engagement obliges me to go."

"And may I ask," rejoined Lady Dunmelraise, in her quick way when she was not pleased at any thing, "may I take the liberty of asking where you are going?"

"Oh, certainly—to Lady Tilney's."

"To Lady Tilney's *party*!" with a marked emphasis on the last word; and then checking herself, and resuming her usual dignity of composure, she added, "I hope you will have an agreeable *soirée*; when one lives out of the world, and grows old, one forgets the delights of these sort of re-unions; but, of course, one must do in London as they do in London; and I believe, like most other things, the habit of attending them becomes a second nature." Lord Albert smiled—it might be in acquiescence, it might be in disdain; and with many good-nights, he slightly touched the hands of Lady Dunmelraise and her daughter, and departed.

There was a silence, an awkward silence; neither liked to express the thought that was uppermost in her mind, for fear of wounding the other. At length Lady Dunmelraise spoke: "It is strange," she said, "to observe the sort of hold which foolish things sometimes obtain over sensible men. The class of persons with whom Lord Albert seems now to be living, are not those I should have conceived that he would ever have selected; but fashion leads young people to do a thousand silly things, which they repent when their ripened judgment shews them in their true colours; and to say truth, I think Lord Albert's manners altogether have not gained by foreign travel. But I suppose I must not express such treason to you, Adeline?" Lady Adeline tried to smile, as she replied:

"I have hardly had time to judge;" and Lady Dunmelraise turned the discourse rather on the associates of Lord Albert than on himself.

"The persons," she said, "he named to us as having been at Restormel, and with whom he now appears so much engaged, are those who live entirely for this world: and not even for the most dignified employments or pursuits of this present existence. Fortune, health, and morals, are all likely to become the prey of a voracious appetite for pleasure; and when we live only to pleasure, we lose all title to being rational souls, and make a wreck of happiness. I am willing to hope and believe, that many are ensnared to tread this Circean circle who are in ignorance of what it leads to; who see in it only a brilliant phantom of amusement, a glittering *ignis fatuus* that pleases their fancy, but which, alas! I fear, too frequently leads them on, till some entanglement of fortune, or virtue, levels them with its worse members; and from which it is a mercy indeed if they ever escape."

Lady Adeline had listened to her mother with an interest that made her shudder. "And is it, indeed," she cried, "in such a set that Albert is thrown!" while the paleness of her countenance expressed the anguish of her mind.

"I trust not, my dearest child. I do not mean to say, for I have no right so to say, that Lord Albert is habitually one of this set;—heaven forbid!—but that he frequents their society appears evident. However, let us not think evil before it actually occurs; let us judge dispassionately, and see for ourselves. You are now, my love, to enter into the great world under an excellent and loving guide; and having warned you, I leave your own good sense to do the rest." Lady Adeline sighed heavily, and did not seem able at all to rally her spirits. "Now, love, let us turn to lighter matters," said Lady Dunmelraise, "and consider the arrangements of your presentation dress."

"I should prefer its being as simple as possible," said Lady Adeline, "and the rest I leave entirely to your, and," she added hesitatingly, "to Lord Albert's tastes." Her mother shortly after proposed retiring for the night, and trembled as she saw how deeply her daughter's happiness seemed to depend on Lord Albert, perceiving that she referred every trifle to his arbitration.

When he left South Audley Street to go to Lady Tilney's supper party, Lord Albert ran over again in his mind the occurrences of the day, and in Lady Adeline's silence, her manner, her looks, he thought he read an indifference towards himself, which at once piqued and wounded him. In all that had fallen from Lady Dunmelraise, in all that he could gather from *her* manner towards himself, he could not fix on any thing unkind or unjust; but from the consciousness of his own conduct not having been what it ought, his heart was ill at ease, and he knew not with what right he felt angry; but yet he did so feel, and was tempted to inveigh against the fickleness of woman, while a thought of Mr. Foley obtruded itself among all the rest, and shewed him an imaginary rival.

"Can all this," he asked himself, "be only preparatory to her breaking off her engagement altogether?"

Such was the mood of mind in which Lord Albert entered Lady Tilney's drawing-rooms, and as hardly any of the invited were as yet come from the Opera, he had leisure unmolested to walk through them. They were brilliantly lighted, and filled with all the rifled sweets of the green-house; sweets, which seem but ill suited in their fresh purity for the scene they were brought to adorn.

While the apartments were still empty, he had an opportunity of examining some of the works of art with which they were decorated. He stopped opposite to a Claude, which was certainly a contrast to the feelings of his own mind. The glowing sunrise, the dancing wave, the palace of the Medici, the business of a sea-port, conveyed him in idea to the Pitti Palace. "Often as that subject has been repeated," he said, turning to Mr. Francis Ombre, "by the same pencil, it is always new, always redolent of repose and pleasure; the scintillating sunbeams are still emblematic of that dancing of the heart, which in the morning of our days gilds every thing with beauty: no, there is no after-pleasure which can equal the sunrise of existence; and if ever picture conveyed a moral truth, the pictures of Claude most assuredly have this power."

"Yes," replied Mr. Ombre, "I love to sun myself at a Claude, it is the only sun one does see in this climate." Lord Albert passed on, sighing as he went, and his attention was again arrested by an antique bust of Psyche: "What refinement of tenderness in the eyelid; what soul in the curvature of the lip! how the line swells, and then is lost again in the almost dimpling roundness of the chin! how child-like, and yet how replete with meaning, the turn of the head and neck! it is at once the bud, the flower, the fruit of beauty amalgamated and embodied in the marble."

It was indeed an emblem of soul. And of whom did it remind Lord Albert? Of his own Adeline. His own! there was an electric touch in the thought—was she *indeed still his own*, or had he lost her for ever? Lady Hamlet Vernon had stood unperceived by him, watching him for some previous minutes, and by that sense which never fails to inform a woman in love, she felt certain from his manner of looking at the Psyche, that it conveyed more to interest him than any mere ideas of *virtù* could possibly do.

Her agitation was extreme, and she could scarcely master it so as to wear a semblance of composure; at length, though the part she had to play was a difficult one, she determined on fulfilling her assignation; and having previously decided how she should manage what she had to do, she went up to him, and at the very moment he was asking himself whether or not he had lost Adeline for ever, a soft voice awoke him to a sense of who and where he was: he turned round and beheld Lady Hamlet Vernon. The recognition of any one whom we believe has an interest in us when the heart feels desolate, is a powerful cordial to the spirits.

Lord Albert greeted her with an animation of pleasure that he was scarcely himself aware of, and which elicited from her an answering sentiment of kindness, that at once cheered and gave him new life. "I have much to say to you," he whispered; "let us sit down in yonder alcove, which is unoccupied, and where we may have an opportunity of speaking unheard by others." He offered her his arm, which she accepted, and they moved to that part of the apartment. At the same instant Lady Glenmore entered, leaning on her husband's arm, and a crowd followed which filled the room. Among these, Mr. Leslie Winyard and Lady Tenderden were conspicuous personages: but Lady Glenmore was the *nouveauté du jour*. When Georgina Melcomb was an unmarried girl, nobody looked at her, or thought about her; but now that she was to play a part, and in her turn become a card to play in the game of fashion, all eyes were fixed upon her. At this moment she was the very picture of innocent happiness, and in the countenance of her husband shone the reflection of her own felicity. There is something in that sort of happiness which involuntarily inspires respect, and to all hearts that are not dead to nature, there is awakened a simultaneous sensation of pleasure.

But yet there are serpents in the world, who, envious of

such pure bliss, seek only its destruction. "Really," said Mr. Leslie Winyard to Lady Tenderden, "that is a fine-looking creature!" speaking of Lady Glenmore as she stood talking with animation to her husband, "and when she has rubbed off a little of her coarseness, and become somewhat less conjugally affected, I don't know but what I may do her the honour to talk to her sometimes myself." Lady Tenderden laughed as she replied,

"There is no saying how condescending you may become— but when do you intend to begin? don't you see that if she is allowed to go on in this way, she will never get out Of it? and as I have undertaken her education myself, I do beg that you will by some contrivance unhook her from Lord Glenmore, and leave me to engage his attention while I make my pupil over to you for the evening, *vraiment ça vaut la peine;* only *la jeune Ladi est tant soit peu maussade et il faut la mettre sur le bon chemin.*"

"With all my heart; if you will only begin the attack I will follow it up."

"*Allons donc,*" she replied, taking his arm and going towards the Glenmores.

The usual nothings of common-place talk, the unmeaning greetings, and the self-same observations on singers and dancers which have been made a hundred times before, opened the meditated campaign. "My dear Lord Glenmore," said Lady Tenderden, "I have long wished to consult you about a *changement de décoration*" (and she looked at Mr. Leslie Winyard) "which I purpose making in my house in town, and I have some thoughts of copying in part the Rotunda-room which is here, only there are some objections to be made to it, which I wish to avoid if possible, and I am desirous that you should assist me with your perfection of taste; have the kindness for a moment to come with me—

but I could not think of giving Lady Glenmore that trouble. There, Mr. Winyard, while I run away with my lord, do you make the *preux chevalier*, and defend Lady Glenmore from all dangers."

So saying, she passed her arm through Lord Glenmore's and led him away. Lady Glenmore looked for a moment as if she intended to follow, and even half rose from her chair for that purpose; but the lessons Lady Tenderden had given her about not seeming to pursue her husband recurred to her, and she sat down again, blushing and breathless, and evidently discomposed. Mr. Leslie Winyard enjoyed the scene: "shall I call Lord Glenmore back again?" he asked, after fixing his eyes upon her maliciously, "or will you allow me to conduct you to him?" and he smiled, evidently in ridicule at her awkwardness. But she was not a fool, though ignorant of the ways of the world; and in a few minutes she recovered herself, and spoke uncommonly well on common-place topics, to the astonishment of her hearer: she even passed upon the set to which he belonged some very stinging remarks, the more so from their being uttered as if unconscious that they were so, or that he was one of the persons to whom they applied.

"Do you know," said he, gazing at her with looks of admiration, "do you know you are a very extraordinary personage? Suffer me to say that this is all very well in joke, but if you are *serious* in your opinions, we must undergo a great revolution, or we shall not be at all able to live with you. I do not pretend," he said, "to decide who is in the right or who is in the wrong, but I am very certain of one thing, a change must take place somewhere, if your ideas of things in general are correct." Lady Glenmore replied, "that she was very certain her ideas would *not* change;" to which he rejoined, "*nous verrons.*"

At that moment a move in the room announced that every

one was going to supper, and the doors were thrown open into an adjoining apartment, towards which there was a general rush. Lady Glenmore again cast her eye anxiously around, but in vain—her husband was not to be seen.

"Allow me," said two or three young men, offering their arm to her, "to hand you to supper," and in the confusion she took that of Mr. Leslie Winyard. "But," he observed, "you seem so uneasy, that if you will allow me, I will merely see you agreeably placed, and go in quest of this envied Lord Glenmore."

"You are very good," she replied, "but I cannot think of giving you that trouble."

"Oh dear, I beg you will not mention it; and the mission is so new a one, that I am particularly proud to be employed in executing it."

"How, new? Is there any thing extraordinary in wishing to know whether one's husband chooses one should go home, or whether he stays supper or not?"

"Yes, Lady Glenmore! most new! most wonderful! But I do not think it is a fashion that will generally take. But here is a table with some seats unoccupied. Will you allow me to recommend your availing yourself of it? It seems to be the choice of the chosen; here is Lady Hamlet Vernon, and Lord D'Esterre, and the Boileaus, and the Ellersbys, and Mr. Spencer Newcomb; do take this seat, and I will go in quest of your lord and *master*. But see, he has not fallen into any of the whirlpools or quicksands that you seem to apprehend for him in these dangerous regions, for by all that is fortunate there he is next to Lady Tenderden."

"Where?" cried Lady Glenmore, looking eagerly around.

"The third table from us, just behind Lady Baskerville; however, if you are still *uneasy*, you have only to command me."

"No, it is his intention to remain for supper, and all is well, for if he had wanted me he would have sought for me."

"Always depend upon that. And now what shall I help you to?" Lady Glenmore, in her own mind, was not at all satisfied as to the danger of whirlpools and quicksands, though they were of another sort from those Mr. Winyard had passed his jokes on; but again Lady Tenderden's advice recurred to her, which had acquired consequence from Lord Glenmore's opinion of that lady, and she endeavoured to enter into the conversation of those around her. It was a sort of dead language as yet to her ears, but she could perceive that, under disguise, many allusions were made to herself, and to her untutored behaviour, which checked her natural flow of spirits, and she gradually became silent, and could no longer conceal her anxious impatience to be once more safe under her husband's wing. The very first person that arose afforded her an opportunity of doing so likewise, and making a sign to Lord Glenmore, she waited for him in the door-way. He was not long before he joined her, and with apparently mutual satisfaction they once more found themselves together. This difference, however, existed in their feelings, that Lord Glenmore, though honourable himself, and incapable of thinking really ill of others, however he might consider them trifling, yet from habit and the manners of the world, had not an idea of watching his wife's conduct in public.

Lord Glenmore's character has been already described; but it has not perhaps been sufficiently explained how very much his guileless unsuspecting nature laid him open to become the prey of others who were the reverse. Let no man cast a young wife (unprepared for the dangers she will meet with) upon the licentious intercourse of the world of *ton*, nor leave her, unguarded by his presence and authority, to stem the tide of vice which may steal in upon her unawares. It is a husband's duty to be the guide and support of his wife; and, without tyranny, but with the determined rectitude of tender solicitude, to watch over their mutual interests. The maxim so often quoted, that "the wife whom a man can doubt is not worthy of his regard," is not always a true one. Every mortal is liable to err—and why should woman, the weaker sex, be cast upon the world, and committed to its dangers, without stay or support from her natural guardian and protector?

The fact is, it is a maxim often resorted to in idleness or indifference, and is more frequently an apology for bad conduct in those who make it, than arising from any true nobility of soul or any moral or religious principle. Lord Glenmore, from living in the midst of the world of fashion, and from never having (a rare instance) been spoiled by such a life, was less aware than any human being perhaps of the danger to which he was exposing his young wife. Had any body told him the terms upon which she was to be admitted as one of the *élite* of *ton*, in plain language, he would have started with disgust and horror from all such association; but, like some few, deceived as he was by specious appearances, he saw nothing in the set but the airiness of fashion, and the folly, at worst, of a few months during the London season; whereas the truth stood thus.—

The husband of an Exclusive must be exclusively given to his own devices, without ever making his wife a party at all concerned in them; unless, indeed, they arrive at that *acmé* of exclusive perfection when they boast to each other of the degrading license of their lives, and tell of their different favourites, comparing the relative merits of these with that of others of the same society. Into the mysteries of an exclusive *coterie* no unmarried woman, that is to say, no girls, are to be admitted—in order that the conversation

81

may be unchecked. The more admirers a married woman has, the higher her reputation amongst them; and it is never quite complete till some one *adorateur* moving in the same circle is the *ami préféré*. If the cavalier be a man of title, power, and wealth, then the lady has *the world—their* world —at her feet. This arrangement ensures the latter (whatever her husband's fortune may be) the advantages of dress and equipage, from which expense *he* is then exonerated; and while he has the credit of keeping up a tasteful establishment, he is exempted from all trouble or thought as to the means by which it is so kept. But as in all communities there are different degrees of distinction, so in this,—those who commence their career have a certain rubicon to pass through before they arrive at such a height of perfection.

The first requisite for a newly-initiated member to know is, how to cut all friends and relations who are not deemed worthy of being of a certain *coterie;*—the next, is to dress after a particular fashion, talk a particular species of language, not know any thing or any person that does not carry the mark of the coterie, and speak in a peculiar tone of voice. To hold any conversation which deserves that name is called being prosy;—to understand any thing beyond the costume of life, pedantic.

Whatever vice or demoralization may exist in character, providing it exist with what they call good taste (that idol of their idolatry), is varnished over. If not approved openly, it is tacitly assented to, and allowed to pass as a venial error; whereas whatever takes place contrary to this *good taste*, though in itself perfectly innocent, tending it may be to virtue rather than vice, is insufferable—not to be named *among them*; and unfits the offending parties from communication with the Exclusives. Indignation expressed at crime is voted vulgar; any natural expression of the

82

feelings, ill-breeding; and right and wrong, in short, consists in being, or not being, *one of the set*. To their choice meetings children dare not invite parents, or brothers and sisters of one another, except under their seal and sign-manual. The husbands and wives, who are members of the association, are invariably persons who have separate interests, separate views, and agree only in this one point, namely, in being a cloak for each other's follies or vices.

It is to be hoped, and indeed may be asserted with truth, that many are ensnared to tread this Circean circle who are in ignorance of what it leads to; who see in it only a brilliant phantasm of pleasure and of pride; an *ignis fatuus* that pleases their fancy; but which terminates too frequently in leading them on, till some entanglement of fortune, or virtue, levels them with its worse members; and from which it is a mercy indeed if they ever escape.

An open defiance of received laws and customs, a coarse career of vicious pleasure, a bold avowal of any illegitimate pursuit, would startle and astound many a wavering mind; but the slow-sapping mischief of this love of exclusiveness, the airy indifference with which all the safeguards of conduct are broken down, the cruel heartlessness which lies concealed under apparently indifferent actions, the artful weaning of the mind from all fixed principle of conduct, these are the means they use; and which, step by step, adulterate the character, indurate the heart, pollute the judgment, and are subversive of every thing that is dignified or amiable in human nature. It is precisely because the evil works so insidiously, and under such a variety of masks (under none more than a placid *insouciance*), a fortuitous occurrence of accidents—that the veil should be drawn aside, and that it should be set forth in its native deformity and danger.

CHAPTER V.

A RURAL EXCURSION.

A BRILLIANT water party had been arranged among the exclusives, to go to Richmond, merely to view the scene; it consisted of the Glenmores, Baskervilles, Lady Tenderden, Comtesse Leinsengen, Lady Tilney, Lord Boileau, Sir William Temple, Lord De Chere, Mr. Winyard, Mr. Spencer Newcomb, Comte Leinsengen, and a few other young men of their set.

When the day arrived, Lord Glenmore told his wife that as he was on a committee of the House, he should not be able to accompany her.

"Then I would far rather not go myself."

"Do not be so childish," he said; "for as we could not, at all events, be together, you might just as well be at Richmond as here; and the day is beautiful, so that I hope you will have a pleasant excursion." Lady Glenmore sighed, and hung her head, while a tear came into her eye.

"What is the matter, love?—Has any thing vexed you?—is it any thing which I can remedy?—You know you have only to speak, and your wishes are my laws." He pressed her fondly to his breast as he said this, and she replied:

"Nothing; nothing vexes me, except that we are hardly ever together, as it seems to me—or never, but when in public; and I long for the time when we shall be in the country, and that all our occupations will be mutual; when you are not with me, I find more pleasure in music, or in reading, than in going to parties: for nobody cares for me; and I am sure I return the compliment."

"Nay, my sweet Georgina, this is really nonsense. Are you not courted and paid attention to by every one in the most marked manner?"

"Do not mistake me," she replied; "I have not explained what I mean. As to outward attentions of politeness, oh! yes, I receive them in abundance; but what I intended to make you understand is, that the things I take interest in, and the pleasures I have in view, seem so entirely different from those of the generality of the set I live in, that there is nothing left for me to say; and I often observe that when I do speak, my conversation is either laughed at, or they stare at me as if they did not believe I was serious."

Lord Glenmore smiled, and loved his innocent little wife a thousand times the more for her unsophisticated sweetness; nevertheless, as he was likely always to have a part to play in the great world, he could not help wishing that his wife should be able, without putting any force upon her inclinations, to do so likewise. He therefore said, and speaking rather more seriously than he had done: "Retain always, dearest Georgina, this youth and purity of character; but, for my sake, learn, my love, to endure an intercourse with others who may be of a less pure nature than yourself; but who are yet, from your situation and circumstances, likely to be those with whom you must naturally associate: to please me, then, my dearest Georgina, begin from to-day: put on all your smiles, and let me hear that you are the envy of the women, and the admiration of the men. Remember, love, to *please me*."

"Any thing to please you," she replied; and she decorated

herself with more than usual care. Just as her toilette was about to be completed, Lord Glenmore entered her room with a quantity of lilies of the valley. "Here," he said, "I have brought you your favourite flowers; wear them, love, and let their fragrance remind you of the donor." All this lover-like attention enchanted the person to whom it was addressed, and her eyes sparkled with unwonted brilliancy, and her cheeks were tinged with the glow of pleasure as she fastened her *bouquet* in her breast. Lord Glenmore, proud of such a wife, as well he might be, handed her into her carriage, and she drove to Lady Tilney's, where the party were to assemble to go to Whitehall stairs.

When she entered the room she found nobody yet arrived; a servant made Lady Tilney's apology, saying she should be dressed shortly. Having played a few airs on the piano-forte, she took up a novel, and was busily employed in its pages when Mr. Leslie Winyard was announced. Lady Glenmore felt embarrassed in his presence, she knew not why, but there was something of fear and flutter that came over her whenever he approached, which she could not command. She arose and curtseyed; and then, as though she had payed him too marked a distinction, she remained awkwardly standing, as though she had taken that position by accident —not in honour of him.

All this was not unobserved by Mr. Winyard. He was too well practised in the ways of women's hearts not to read her's at a glance. At least he occasioned emotion, no matter what emotion. He was not to be seen with indifference— that was enough for him; and he despaired not of turning it to his own advantage. This advantage, however, was not, in the present instance, to be obtained by a *coup de main*; and assuming an air of polite, but frigid *nonchalance*, he accosted Lady Glenmore with an expression of surprise at finding her the first-arrived person; and then examined one of the miniatures which hung in a glass cabinet. Lady Glenmore soon recovered her composure, and entered into conversation by asking some of those questions which are merely the opening of conversation. "Yes, I like music," said Mr. Winyard, in answer to one of her questions; "it is one of the very few things which is worth giving one's-self any trouble about. I once learned to sing; the only thing I ever learned." Lady Glenmore laughed; and as her own ingenuous manner returned, she evinced that propensity to being amused by the present moment, which is so natural and so pleasing in youth.

"Will you do me the honour to sing a duet with me?"

"Oh! certainly," she said; and turning over some music which lay scattered on the instrument, she added, "Oh! here is that delightful little duet, '*Sempre più*' which, though not new, is always charming." Mr. Leslie Winyard had a sort of shuddering at the idea that, notwithstanding her general elegance, she might excruciate his ears by an open English pronunciation, and a drawl by way of sentiment; but he had embarked in the danger, and fortunately there was no one in the way to hear if his own talent should be marred. He therefore courageously opened the music leaf; and Lady Glenmore, having touched a few chords, gave an assurance that better things were in store. Nor did she disappoint the promise; her sweet, rich-toned voice had been tutored by Italian taste, and swelled or sunk to every intonation, with a delicacy of feeling which could not be surpassed; the *sempre più t'amo* was uttered in the purest enunciation of the language; and Mr. Leslie Winyard thought, if it were only addressed to him, it would be a triumph, which the world he had lived in had not yet afforded. Lady Tilney entered the room while they were yet singing.

"I am glad to find you have not been tired," she said, "waiting for me. I beg you a thousand pardons, Lady

Glenmore; but really I had so many things to do to-day—notes, those terrible time destroyers; and then the last number of the Edinburgh Review, together with Mr. Kirchoffer's last work, have so entirely occupied me, I totally forgot how the hours flew past, till Argenbeau told me that you were arrived. However, I hope you find the instrument in good order. Mr. Winyard sings like an angel; and I make no doubt," (looking at him, to ask how far she was right in the assertion) "Lady Glenmore does so likewise."

Mr. Winyard said, "I assure you, Lady Tilney, *que voilà ce que l'on appelle chanter*," indicating Lady Glenmore with a movement of his head, "I had no idea any thing not of the Land of Song could sing in that manner."

"Well, really, you astonish me; why Lady Glenmore keeps all her perfections to herself! But she must really be drawn out, and not suffered to hide her talents in obscurity."

At this moment Lady Tenderden and the Baskervilles entered, and shortly after the remainder of the company. "Well, it is time we should be gone, if we mean to see Richmond," observed Mr. Spencer Newcomb, "though I believe *eating* Richmond is fully as interesting, and candle-light at any time is better worth seeing than the sun-light; are you not of my opinion, Lady Glenmore?" He addressed himself in preference to her, because he thought she was new enough to be astonished, and astonishment was an homage paid to his power which he well knew he could not extract from any of the rest of the company.

"Both are good," replied Lady Glenmore, "in their proper season."

"A philosophical answer!" cried Sir William; "you did not expect that, did you, Newcomb?"

"No, it is too wise for me," he said, "for it leaves me nothing to say—it is a truism; *messieurs et mesdames, je vous avertie,* that as I do not like the evening fogs of the river I cannot postpone my departure. Lord Baskerville, Mr. Winyard, will you come with me? I have a *voiture a quatre places,* and any lady may come that likes." Mr. Leslie Winyard bowed and whispered Lady Glenmore, "would she go?" Lady Tenderden whispered her on the other side, "by all means go, my dear Lady Glenmore, and I will arrange my party in your carriage."

Lady Tenderden's advice was not to be slighted, and Lady Glenmore accordingly accepted Mr. Leslie Winyard's offered arm, and followed Comtesse Leinsengen, who treating her as nobody, as she was generally wont to do every one whom she dared, she entered her carriage and drove off. At Whitehall-stairs they found their boat waiting, the best barge, the most knowing bargemen, and all things in exquisite order—they take their places, and, a band of music following, glide down the stream, and are, or appear to be, in the most harmonious of humours.

"What is become of Glenmore to-day?" asked Lord Gascoigne.

"I am sorry to say he was obliged to be on a committee, and I feel so lonely without him, half my pleasure is gone," replied Lady Glenmore. The men looked at one another—the ladies tittered; there was a pause, and the speaker felt sadly embarrassed, she knew not why. Lady Tenderden whispered to her as they leaned over the boat-side:

"That was a very injudicious speech of your's, my dear; you must learn not to *affiché* these tendernesses; for if you really feel them nobody cares, and people in general only imagine you affect them by way of being singular."

Poor Lady Glenmore made no answer; but was again convinced that she should never like a society in which she was to be so perfectly unnatural. Mr. Leslie Winyard, who saw at a single glance the truth and freshness of Lady Glenmore's character, was certain that it would not do to attempt to gain her good graces by any common-place mode of attack, such as flattery of the person, or intoxicating representations of power, dissipation, and pleasure. He therefore took an opportunity, when the rest of the party were engaged in their own conversation, to approach Lady Glenmore, and having found a seat next to her, he commenced a discourse which he conceived would be more to her taste. Music afforded him an opening; it was a subject on which he spoke elegantly and well, and she listened with pleased attention.

"After all," he observed, "where science and taste have done their utmost to produce perfection, and without these guides certainly nothing will do; even after they have lent their assistance, there is a third ingredient which is *given* only, and cannot be *acquired*, without which there will ever remain a flatness, an *ineffectiveness*, if I may so speak, which renders the whole vapid and inefficient—I mean feeling; and there, indeed, you must know, Lady Glenmore, that you are not wanting." He fixed his eyes on her with an expression which made her blush; but she replied smiling:

"How can *you* know that, Mr. Winyard?"

"Did I not hear you a short time ago sing '*Sempre piu t'amo*'?"

"Oh," she replied, "you judge by that?"

"And can I appeal to a more convincing proof of what I assert? But if I needed any other proof, surely the words, and the look which accompanied the words, when you expressed your regret at Lord Glenmore not being of the party to-day, would be an undoubted corroboration of the fact."

"Oh, that was natural," she said; "it would have been odd could I have done otherwise. But real feeling is a much deeper seated quality than can be judged of by singing a song, or a passing impulse, and I do not own that you can know any thing about me or my feelings."

"Perhaps not," replied Mr. Leslie Winyard, looking grave and humble; "may it be my good fortune to know more of these, and to have the honour and advantage of improving my acquaintance with you."—Here a louder laugh than was usual among the fastidious in manners, interrupted this *tête-à-tête*; "will you not allow us to benefit by the wit?" asked Mr. Winyard.

"Oh," said Lady Tenderden, "it is only that Sir William Temple fell asleep, and asked, when he was awoke, for some more maids of honour."—"To be sure," he said, "what does one go to Richmond for, but to eat those exquisite compositions. If all maids of honour were like them, I am sure their race would be more in vogue than it is. I would give a hundred or two to have the receipt, for notwithstanding that I have brought my cook disguised *en valet de chambre* a thousand times, he never could find out the secret; neither has he been able, with all his art, to produce any precise *fac-simile*."

"Ah!" exclaimed Lord Gascoigne, "that is the true spirit of philanthropy; a hundred or two for a receipt to make cheesecakes! while we have such men in the state we need not be under any apprehension that the arts and sciences will fail."

"Yes, arts and sciences, my Lord Gascoigne; for I affirm that the pleasures of the table require one to be an adept, both in order to procure and preserve them in perfection. Who will deny that the cultivation and use of the animals, and vegetables, and elements, that are employed, do not include all these, not to speak of the *main d'œuvre*."

"I am not disputing the fact," said Lord Gascoigne; "why did you address yourself to me? On the contrary, I am so well convinced of it, that I pay my cook a hundred a year: but the rascal threatens to leave me if I do not raise his wages."

"I cannot be surprised at that," said Lord Baskerville, "for I give mine two, and he is only a second-rate performer."

"It is vastly extravagant," cried Lady Tilney; "however, one need not do it if one does not chuse; and, after all, it is not too much to pay a man to become a salamander."

"Oh," cried the Comtesse Leinsengen, "*ils son fait au feu ces gens-là*, they are good for nothing else, and if you were not to yield to them, you would have them for half de money; but you are all *des dupes* in England. You think the more you pay, de grander you are, that is the truth."

"Well, my dear Comtesse," rejoined Lord Baskerville, "that is all very well to say, but I am certain that you never would get any body to serve you if you did not pay him well; and I must declare that I had rather give a hundred or two more to my cook, than to any other servant in my house; for one's whole domestic comfort depends upon one's cook, don't you think so, Temple?"

"I was always of opinion that you were a wise man, and I am now confirmed in that opinion. Most indubitably one's cook is the great nucleus upon which one's whole existence, mental and physical, depends; for if you eat of a bad greasy ragoût, the *physique* immediately suffers, and then bilious hypochondria ensues, and one's friends are the victims of one's indigestion; and all the economy of life, in short, goes wrong, if there is a failure in that department."

"Nobody has ever denied," observed Mr. Spencer Newcomb, "*que le bonheur est dans l'estomac*, and that happiness depends very much on what one eats—and what one eats depends upon the cook. I hold it to be an incontrovertible maxim, *que le bonheur des bonheurs* is to have a *cordon bleu* at one's command—even the ladies will agree with me."

"Certainly," said Lady Baskerville, "I account it to be one of the requisites of life."

"Yes," rejoined Mr. Winyard; "for a lady ought to appreciate the beauty of every thing, even of a *poulet santé aux truffes*; and though I cannot endure a woman to have what is vulgarly called a good appetite—a sort of beef and cabbage voraciousness—I like her to know the various flavours and high-wrought refinements of the palate. Indeed, I am sure she is always vulgar if she does not. But here, we are nearly at the landing-place; and now let us hope to put our theories in practice, and find in this *rural* retreat a change of viands to recreate and stimulate our somewhat palsied palates."

As the ladies were gathering up their shawls and reticules, Lady Glenmore stooped down to arrange a part of her dress, and the lilies of the valley her husband had given her fell into the water. She made an exclamation, and attempted to catch them, but a breeze bore them beyond her reach. "Oh my nosegay! I would not lose it for the world," she cried.

Mr. Leslie Winyard looking in her face, and seeing that she was eager in her wish to recover the flowers, hastily darted from another part of the boat; and in making an effort to catch them, lost his balance, and fell into the water. As they were literally on the shore, there was no sort of danger, besides that of getting a ducking; but he thought it might avail him something in Lady Glenmore's favour: nor was he mistaken. Seeing him floundering in the water, she cried out, "for God's sake save his life!" and while he made the most of the awkwardness of his situation, he kept brandishing the lilies with one hand, and would not suffer any body to touch them till he delivered them safely to her. She was exceedingly touched by this effort to oblige her, and for the rest of the evening, after he had made a fresh toilette, he reaped the rewards of his gallantry, by finding that Lady Glenmore listened to him with a kind of favourable impression, that he could scarcely have hoped to inspire her with, had not fortune thus favoured him.

During dinner nothing was talked of but the merits of a Richmond party:—"there is surely nothing in the world more beautiful," said Mr. Newcomb, "than the view of Richmond Hill; it is the only *riante* landscape in England; a perfect Claude; and for my part, I never desire to go farther in quest of the picturesque—it is quite a *gentle* scene; no horrors, no rugged rocks or torrents; but a sweet, soft, sylvan composition."

"Enlivened too," observed Sir William Temple, "by stage-coaches, and mail-coaches, and coaches of all sorts, in short; without which I hold all views to be very wearisome things *à la longue*."

"Only made for the eyes of the vulgar, depend upon it," was Lord Baskerville's observation. "Except during the hunting season, the country is hateful; but one may bear a row to Richmond, especially in such company,"—and he bowed to Comtesse Leinsengen.

"The country is all very well," she rejoined, "in a *grande chateau bien remplie de tout ce qu'il y a de mieux en fait de société*; but it makes me shudder to think of being in one of your provinces, in a house in the middle of a shut-up park, with a neighbour or two *pour tout bien*; no no, I am perished with *ennui* but to think of it."

"It makes me shudder too," said Lady Baskerville, smiling at the Comtesse Leinsengen's broken English; "but, in fact, it is what nobody does now-a-days; either the real or the pretended incapacity on the score of fortune for living at the country-seats, as they used to be called, gets rid of all that sort of thing. People live very much now as they used to do in France, I am told, when Paris was the only place in that country which any body lived in."

"Yes," said Mr. Spencer Newcomb, "and as long as the people don't find out that their landlords forsake them, and rack them for their money, which they spend any where rather than in doing them any good, it is very agreeable not to be bored with that sort of useful virtuous life. Long may they continue to administer to our pleasures—they ought certainly to be made for nothing else; but, unfortunately, there came a time in France when these things were all changed, and the vulgars took it into their heads that they were to have their day; and off went heads, and on went caps of liberty, and all things were turned upside down, as every body knows. I wonder now how Lord Baskerville would like to turn groom, and rub down his own horses!"

"Ha! ha! ha!" was echoed around.

"So long as you keep a good whip hand, and de rein in both, you will not be in any danger," cried Comtesse Leinsengen; "you have only to keep down *de canaille*. What sinifie all these schools of learning? dey are the most terrible nonsense; good for nothing but to turn the people's heads, and make them think themselves wiser than their masters; we do not do so in my country. When they learn to sing, they only learn *one note*, so that no single person is independent of anoder, and yet they make excellent concerts; these sort of people should be always kept dat way, so you see dat keeps all quiet, and the country goes on from one age to another all de same."

"Capital," said Winyard, "that is worth putting in print."

"Oh, I am quite of another opinion," cried Lady Tilney; "you must pardon me; but I think that every thing which has not freedom for its basis, must be wrong; let every body have a fair chance of becoming something; above all, let the light of learning shine every where, in every thing; there will always be ways and means of keeping people in their several stations. A country may have all the blessings of liberty, and yet a certain set may exist who shall have a superiority of its own, move in a sphere of its own, and be kept quite apart from the vulgar crowd; there is always a way of managing these things. I uphold liberty and literature; but that is not to say, that your authors and your musicians are to mix with certain societies—quite the contrary. The liberty of the latter will always keep its ground against the intrusion of the former, don't you think so, Sir William?"

"I think, Lady Tilney, that whatever you say must be right; and when you command, I feel always inclined to reply, as some body, I forget who, did to the Queen of France, *si c'est possible c'est déjà fait, si c'est impossible ça ce fera.*"

"I have always thought," rejoined Mr. Spencer Newcomb, "that that speech ought to be the truest that ever was uttered, for it is exactly the sort of thing a lady would like to have said, and I am sure it is the most ingenious that ever was contrived." A walk was now proposed, previous to which the ladies withdrew to the drawing-room.

"Well," said Lady Tenderden, "I think we have had a charming day, do you not Lady Glenmore?"

"Very much so," she replied, "and if only——."

"I will finish the phrase for you—if only Lord Glenmore was here—now my dear, I thought I had warned you not to indulge in that infantine habit of saying always what you think. You cannot conceive what strange ideas men attach to these sort of declarations; they are apt to suppose it is a hint to them to make love to you."

"Impossible!" said Lady Glenmore, colouring.

"Oh, you do not yet know the world, my dear Lady Glenmore. Be advised at first, and then afterwards act for yourself."

"I must beg of you, ladies," interrupted Comtesse Leinsengen, coming up to them, "to patronize a little *modiste* who is newly established, and whom I take under my special protection. She has all her patterns from Paris—dey are of the *premier goût*, and have that particular mark of distinction about them, which dose who are copied from the *feuilles des modes* never so attain. Mademoiselle Dumesnil has promised me never to sell certain things but to certain people; so that one is quite sure of not seeing *le double* of one's own dress on Mrs. Hoffer, or Lady Delafont, which is quite sufficient to make one fall into a syncope, and put one in bad humour for de whole season."

The Ladies smiled, agreed with her, and promised compliance with her wishes. "Mademoiselle Dumesnil's story," continued Comtesse Leinsengen, *"feroit un roman*; it is quite touching, and" (she added in a whisper, as the gentlemen entered the room), "its hero, *le voilà,*" pointing to Mr. Leslie Winyard; then in a low voice she proceeded to give the whole particulars to the two Ladies, Glenmore and Tenderden, who sat next to her.

The gentlemen now expressed their wish to know whether the ladies would not profit by the beauty of the evening to walk out, and the measure being agreed upon, the party was so arranged that Lady Glenmore fell to the lot of Mr. Leslie Winyard, and much as she now felt averse to accept his arm, after the particulars she had just heard from Comtesse Leinsengen, it was impossible for her to refuse without incurring, as she thought, Lady Tenderden's animadversions. Lady Glenmore's silence, however, as they walked along, attracted her companion's particular notice. Something, he conceived, must have occurred, to change her manner so completely since dinner; but Mr. Leslie Winyard was too well versed in intrigue to augur from this circumstance any thing unfavourable to his wishes, because he knew that to have made an impression *quelconque*, was the first step towards attaining his end.

Determined, nevertheless, to ascertain the reason of this alteration in Lady Glenmore's manner, he very cautiously, but very adroitly, contrived to find out that something had been said which she conceived was to his disadvantage; and he could be at no loss to guess of what nature it was, for the affair in which his name had been mixed up, in Comtesse Leinsengen's conversation, was of too recent a date, and too *marquante*, to have escaped the memories even of that thoughtless circle—it was, in short, his last.

With this just apprehension of the fact, therefore, he turned the conversation upon the subject of scandal, which he deprecated bitterly; and, as if instancing the effects of it in regard to a person intimately known to himself, gave a totally different, but very plausible, interpretation of the exact story, which Lady Glenmore had heard detailed half an hour before by Comtesse Leinsengen.

Lady Glenmore had listened to this artful language with considerable interest and surprise. From the generosity of her nature, she felt much pleasure in thinking that the evil she had heard, and which made her uneasy even to be in Mr. Leslie Winyard's society, was totally without foundation. Her manner, therefore, gradually relaxed in rigour towards him; she seemed to have suddenly recovered her spirits, and her conversation flowed naturally without any constraint.

The moment the party returned from their walk she flew up to Lady Tenderden, and referring to the previous conversation of Comtesse Leinsengen, repeated that which she had just heard from Mr. Leslie Winyard, and which she conceived to be his interpretation of his own story; commenting, as she related it, on the injurious effects of speaking evil of any person without a thorough knowledge of the fact. Lady Tenderden foresaw, that were all this carried back to Lord Glenmore, many impediments would arise in fitting Lady Glenmore for their exclusive circle, and bringing her down to a moral level with themselves; she therefore said, after a minute's pause, "I make no doubt the Comtesse Leinsengen has been exceedingly misinformed; but at the same time the less that is said of these matters is always best, on every account; and as Mr. Leslie Winyard is my very particular friend, I shall esteem it a favour, my dear Lady Glenmore, that you do not mention this idle story to Lord Glenmore, who might conceive some prejudice against him, which would make me very unhappy. It is, in fact, of no consequence whatever; but when things of that nature pass through various mouths, they accumulate a consequence in their passage which they have not in themselves; and therefore promise me, dear Lady Glenmore, that you will not mention this matter to any one; besides," she added, looking very mysterious, "you know Lord Glenmore's great interests may be much affected by the Leinsengens; and the knowledge of her having retailed that sort of story, and retailed it under a mistaken point of view, might produce some coolness between them; for you know Lord Glenmore is vastly fond of Mr. Leslie Winyard."

Lady Glenmore did *not* know this, and hardly comprehended any part of the speech; in truth, how should she? But she remembered her husband's having recommended her to take Lady Tenderden's advice, and therefore she determined so to do in the present instance.

Shortly after this conversation, it was put to the vote whether the party should return to town by land or by water; and with the exception of Princess Leinsengen and Lord Baskerville, who preferred a close carriage for fear of damp, the rest agreed to go as they had come. It was soon quite night; but a brilliant moon made the water look very beautiful; and the soft language of Mr. Winyard, as he sat by the side of Lady Glenmore in the boat, fashioned in its phrase to the taste of his hearer, appeared to her in unison with the scene, and she thought him the only one of the party who was at all amusing, or had given a colouring of any interest to the hours she had passed with them.

Arrived at Whitehall, Lady Tenderden proposed their adjourning to her house, where supper was prepared; but Lady Glenmore, uneasy at a longer absence from home and her husband's society, determined for once to be firm in her refusal; and stepping into her carriage, which awaited her, drove at once home. On her arrival there, however, she was doomed to sustain an unexpected disappointment, as she found a note from Lord Glenmore, dated from the House; in which he told her not to be uneasy if he were late, for that the business of the morning was likely to be followed by a protracted debate on an important question. Lady Glenmore sighed over this note as she perused it; and, tired with the day's excursion, yet not sufficiently composed for rest, she experienced that listlessness of mind, which admits not of any active exertion, and yet affords no satisfactory contemplation whereon to dwell.

Lord Glenmore's attention happened to be at this moment directed to a high post under government, which it was more than probable he would attain. But could he have dreamt that in this pursuit he was neglecting the duties of private life, and casting forth an inexperienced young person, unprotected, amid all the dangers of a pleasure-loving world, he would have left all else to guide her through the perils to which he now so frequently left her exposed. How often does it happen, in various instances, that in the blindness of human wishes, we hurry to the goal of our desires—even those which we deem innocent and praiseworthy; but which, when suffered to lead us on, without a reference to a higher power, never fail to *mislead*, and prove fallacious when obtained. Yes, this is that self-pride of reason, which, confiding too much in its own merits, and not acting under the reliance of a superintending Providence, even when on the point of realizing its fondest hopes, finds it has grasped at a shadow; and to an ideal good, sacrificed a permanent happiness.

Had Lord Glenmore paused to reflect, and had recourse to that unerring light, which never dazzles to betray—his steps would have been guided by unfailing wisdom, and he would have found his chief happiness in his chief duty; whereas he pursued the phantom ambition; he did not consider that the necessary consequence which must follow an official occupation, was his leaving his young wife without a natural protector, amid scenes that were any thing but safe; and he was desirous that she, too, should play her part, and by those graces and influences which have such sway over the destinies of men and of empires, take an interest and acquire a power in that vaulting game of ambition in which he himself delighted to engage. He considered not how often he must leave her through the day, and the greater part of the night, to run this hazardous career, at an age when caution sleeps and passions are awake, and in the midst of a set which, though certainly not wholly devoid of some unblemished characters, was yet, generally speaking, in its whole tendency perilous to the pure and domestic virtues—a woman's only true glory.

Yet on this precipice was Lady Glenmore placed, without one real friend to whom she could look for genuine advice or succour. Her mother's (Lady Melcomb) absence from town prevented that natural tie, and had she been there it would have proved the business of the exclusives to have prevented that free and happy intercourse, both on the principle of not allowing any aged person to mar the brilliancy of their set, as well as that of excluding all those who might see through the drift of the society. On Lady Melcomb's part it was too early in the day to have any suspicion of the work of mischief which was carrying on to separate her from her daughter, and thus was Lady Glenmore like a lovely lamb amidst ravening wolves.

Scarcely had she been received amongst them, when Mr. Leslie Winyard, being at the moment *desœuvré*, conceived that she was just put in his way as a fit play-thing for the hour, and without the least scruple he determined she should swell the list of his conquests, already as numerous as those of Don Giovanni in all lands. He took no pains to conceal this design from any one save herself, and his intentions served many of the set as a topic of conversation, a fit subject for betting on: "how would Glenmore take the thing; would he be a wise man or a fool—put on the cap which fitted him with a good grace, or make grimaces at it?" Such is the license with which the most serious delinquencies were talked over, and though when set down on paper they may seem exaggerated, yet certainly the fact is not in the least so; only people start at things and actions when called by their right names, which under the title of venial errors, youthful indiscretions, and the sanction of custom and habit, are certainly tolerated, if not commended; *tacitly* approved, if not openly avowed. Ought not such a desperate system to be analyzed? Ought not language to pourtray in its strongest terms those deeds and those manners which, under the semblance of polite terms, and fictitious representation, and deceptive elegancies, pass current as being harmless or indifferent.

Let those whose hearts have bled on the shrine of fashion and of *ton*—who have mourned the loss of all that was valuable in character, or beautiful in mental existence, sacrificed to the insatiable appetite of pleasure, the degrading occupations of frivolous pursuit, —let *them* say if colours can be too deep, or language too strong, to paint so destructive an evil as that of the whole false, futile system of the exclusiveness of *ton*.

Lady Glenmore was evidently one of those persons marked out to become its victim, and when the character of Mr. Leslie Winyard is taken into account, as being the man who attempted above all others to lead her to her ruin, it cannot be wondered at, circumstanced as she was, that the pit of degradation yawned at her feet. Mr. Winyard was one of those who to the gentlest manners united the hardest of hearts: he had not, perhaps, always merited such a description; but the being who lives entirely for pleasure, becomes gradually hardened to every natural sentiment, and selfishness is the invariable consequence of a life of idle dissipation. From selfishness springs every other evil, and as it is the meanest of all principles of action, when considered in the baldness of the term, so it is, perhaps, the most common, and the one which above all others no person will like to avow—no, not even Mr. Leslie Winyard.

Yet he was a man who, after having by every sort of riot and debauchery ruined himself, proceeded to ruin his own mother and sister, bringing the grey hairs of the one to the grave with sorrow, and leaving the other to work out her existence in a situation unfitting her rank, but far more honourable and desirable than the one he filled; yet this was a man, the beauty of whose personal appearance, the refinement of whose manners, the powers of whose understanding and charm of fascination, were calculated to destroy every innocent mind; and it was difficult to arm against such a powerful enemy—a very Proteus in the power of becoming all things at pleasure, and suiting himself precisely to the taste and habits of the victim whom he was insidiously endeavouring to undermine.

What could protect an unsuspecting, youthful mind against such an enemy? Nothing but religion; nothing but that habitual looking for wisdom, where alone it may be found; and perhaps, Lady Glenmore was in this only security fatally defective; she was good and pure, in as much as human nature can be said to be so. And how totally valueless this goodness is, without it rests on a firmer basis, may be seen in her, as in every other person to whom the same vital want attaches: for her character was not built on that rock which when the floods come, and the storm beats, will remain unmoved by them: she had yet the greatest of all lessons to learn, not to depend on *self*.

CHAPTER VI.

RETROSPECTION.

WHEN Lady Hamlet Vernon drew Lord Albert D'Esterre aside, at Lady Tilney's supper party, it was, he conceived, with an intention of explaining to him the words contained in her note at Restormel alluding to Lady Adeline Seymour —and he was confirmed in this idea by the violent agitation which her manner betrayed, although she strove to retain that composure which the circumstances of the time and place particularly demanded. For several minutes after they had sat down, she seemed labouring for breath; and Lord Albert, notwithstanding his own anxiety and impatience felt exceedingly for her distress.

"My dear Lady Hamlet Vernon," he said, "I beseech you be not thus agitated; remember, whatever you have to say, however painful it may be to me to hear, I am certain that it must be from friendly motives alone that you make such communication, and I must always feel grateful to you for your intention; but keep me no longer in suspense I entreat, for I am prepared for whatever you may have to tell me."

"I have nothing to tell you, Lord Albert."

"What do you mean? what, can you possibly intend to disappoint me; and, having so cruelly excited my feelings, cast them back upon me to prey upon themselves? No, I never can believe you so inconsequent; so very—"

"Stay, Lord Albert, and before you condemn, hear me.—It is

106

true I was on the point of betraying a trust—of revealing a secret—of becoming *really dishonourable*—for what? for the sole purpose of befriending you—for the sole purpose of snatching *you* from a danger which it was then time to prevent your falling into; but since that moment is past for ever—since it is now in vain that I should prove useful to you by being false to another, my lips must for ever be sealed."

"Strange and unaccountable mystery! What, you will not tell me—you will not endeavour to warn me against a danger which hangs over me—is this friendship? How *can you* know that the time is past for pointing out to me such danger? How can *you* be so thoroughly acquainted with the events of my life—the secrets of my heart, as first to imagine my fate *was* in your hands, and then suddenly be equally well assured it is so no longer? No, I cannot conceive there is any friendship in such conduct."

"Ah," said Lady Hamlet Vernon, sighing, "I see you are like all your sex; you receive the devotion of a heart as a thing of course; you take into no consideration the pain, the remorse I felt, at the idea of becoming false to a trust for your sake, when I thought that by so doing I might save you from misfortune. And now that I tell you the time is gone by when I might possibly have been of use, even by the sacrifice of my own integrity, you still wish for that sacrifice, although it can avail you nothing:—is this generous?" Lord Albert felt confused; he was even moved by the look, the air, the words of Lady Hamlet Vernon, but still the disappointment wrung his heart, and jealousy, with every other feeling, goaded him on to press for a disclosure of the secret.

"I am not ungrateful, indeed I am not; I feel deeply the kind interest you take in me; but if that interest does not sleep, or

107

rather if it is not extinguished, I still plead to be made acquainted with a circumstance so very nearly affecting my welfare; and when I say that your disclosing it to me would be like keeping it in another casket, surely, surely you will not deny me."

"In this respect, my dear Lord Albert, I alone can be the judge, and even at the risk of losing your good opinion, or rather of losing your friendship for the time being, I must persist in remaining silent." There was a long pause, which was at last interrupted by Lady Hamlet Vernon resuming the conversation.

"Whatever may be your opinion of me, I must, ere our intercourse altogether ceases, touch upon one subject, which I believe to be the prime object of your life, and that to which all your views tend—I mean the noble career which lies open to your ambition; may you pursue it with unbounded success; but remember, that you are not likely to do so if you have any secondary interest to clog and drag you back. If domestic troubles, at least domestic cares, obtrude themselves upon your higher aims, what a terrible hindrance to your plans they must of necessity become. Think well, my dear Lord Albert, of this—for *le roman de la vie* is soon over you know, but life itself goes on to the end; and whatever women do, men should look to that alone with a providing care. We, who are creatures born to suffer (at least all women who live as most women do, the slaves of your sex), we indeed may live upon that illusion, which destroys while it delights; but it is not in your nature to do so; public concerns—public applause—public success—facts, not feelings, must fill up the measure of a man's existence. Think, then, what it is to have these great ends marred, defeated, by some minor power that corrodes and destroys in detail those thoughts, those actions, which, if unshackled by petty duties, would raise you to high consideration and power; but if tied to a partner wholly a stranger to your feelings and pursuits, she must, however amiable in herself, ultimately poison all your happiness."

Lord Albert had listened to Lady Hamlet Vernon without a wish to interrupt her, and with deep and fixed attention, painfully dwelt upon every word she uttered; he could not remain in ignorance of the drift of her words, and they pierced him like swords, yet still he remained silent.

"If," continued Lady Hamlet Vernon, "a woman shares her husband's feelings, enters into his views, goes along with him, not merely from duty but from habit and inclination, in all his interests, then indeed it is possible such a woman might forward, and not impede his prospects; but where habits, principles, and prejudices, have all tended to form a different character, and above all, where bigotry has fastened chains on the mind wholly destructive of any active or useful pursuits, the probability is, that wretchedness to both ensues." Lord Albert no longer affected to misunderstand her, and replied,

"Every thing you have said has been in allusion to my approaching union with Lady Adeline Seymour, an engagement you cannot be ignorant of, as it has been well known to the world in general for some years past. Tell me, I adjure you tell me, to what principles, to what habits do you allude? There is enough in your words to startle and confound me; but there lurks yet an unpronounced sentence in your mind, which I now implore you to declare. If, indeed, the least regard for my happiness ever swayed your breast, be explicit now, for my destiny perhaps hangs on your open sincerity." Lord Albert's thoughts were one chaos of uneasiness and pain; jealousy had fired the train, which set his whole being in a state of anarchy, and he lost all command over himself—all presence of mind, or capability of sifting truth from falsehood. Poor human reason, how weak is it even in the strongest minds! when the passions are roused, who dares to answer for himself, unless a higher power assist him in his hour of need?

"Be composed, be calm," said Lady Hamlet Vernon, "do nothing in haste; suffer me now to drop this subject, and we may resume it at a more favourable opportunity, when you have considered fully the opinions I have now expressed. All I wish you to remember is, that when a man chooses a companion for life, the chief thing to be considered is, not her amiable qualities, but whether they are of a kind which will assimilate with his. The mere obedience which proceeds from duty, will never satisfy a noble nature: no, it is the devotion of a glowing heart which beats in unison — a mind capable of sharing in the plans and pursuits of an aspiring nature, unwarped by prejudice, unobscured by fanaticism; above all, a heart that is wholly and undividedly its own."

Lord Albert, in listening to these words, unconsciously compared the happiness of being united to such a woman as the one he now heard and beheld, to that of the pure but infantine mind of Adeline Seymour. "Besides," he thought, "is she so pure? has no preference for another, usurped the allegiance which she owes wholly to me? Has George Foley not become more necessary to her than myself?" And while these imaginations, and such as these passed rapidly to and fro in his mind, his eyes were rivetted on Lady Hamlet Vernon, whose exceeding beauty heightened by the expression of an interest for himself which he never before had seen so visibly betrayed, made him say, in a tone and manner not devoid of a similar feeling,

"Oh! Lady Hamlet Vernon, you who can paint happiness so well — you who know to distinguish, with such enchanting delicacy, those shades of felicity which my warm imagination has figured to be the charm of married life, do not with a pertinacity unlike yourself, withhold from me the secret on which my fate depends, and either be my guardian-angel or—"

"Hold, I beseech you in my turn; I have already told you that I cannot fully impart all I know—I may not, must not be explicit. But this much I will reveal to you, providing you swear to keep the secret, and never to probe me further."

"Oh yes, I swear I will never betray so generous a friend; I will never search further into what you wish that I should not know."

"Well, then," Lady Hamlet Vernon replied, after a pause, and trembling with excessive emotion, "for the sake of the great, the deep interest I feel for you, and have felt since I first knew you, receive this pledge and earnest of my friendship;" saying which, she placed a ring in his hand, and added at the same time in a low distinct voice, "you can never be happy with Lady Adeline Seymour."

There are blows and shocks which strike at the very vitality of existence—who has not felt these before he has numbered many years? and such was the power of these words on Lord Albert, that he remained for some minutes motionless; their sound vibrated in his ear long after the sound itself had ceased; for strange it is, though true, that we can sometimes endure to think what we scarcely can bear to hear uttered. In the one case the thought seems not to be embodied in reality; in the latter it has received existence, and appears actually stamped with the seal of certainty.

At length, however, he had summoned his reason to his aid, and was about to speak further to Lady Hamlet Vernon, when, interrupted by the quick succeeding questions of many of the company who were passing the room in which they sat to go to supper, Lord Albert offered his arm

111

mechanically to Lady Hamlet Vernon, and they followed in the train of others. The noise and gaiety and brilliancy of the scene could not for a moment take Lord Albert out of himself; one idea, one image engrossed him, and all the surrounding persons and circumstances glanced before his eye or came to his ear, with the glitter and the buzz of undistinguishable lights and sounds. He went through the forms of the place and scene with the precision of an automaton, and when the supper ended he followed Lady Hamlet Vernon about like her shadow, sometimes absorbed in the deepest concentration of thought, sometimes endeavouring to revert to their former conversation, which had been so abruptly, and to him so unopportunely broken off; eager to renew its discussion, as well as to elicit a disclosure (regardless of his solemn promise) of that part of the subject on which she refused all explanation.

In both, however, he wholly failed; and having been obliged, although reluctantly, to part from her for that time, he handed Lady Hamlet Vernon to her carriage and bent his way home. He felt it a relief to be alone, in order to take a review more collectedly of what was passing in his own breast: but yet, when he commenced the task, he found a contradiction of thoughts and feelings which were so involved that for a time he yielded to them, and they alternately swayed him in opposite directions, without his being able to come to any decision.

On considering the length of time, and the intimate footing on which Mr. Foley had lived at Dunmelraise (notwithstanding the peculiar circumstances in which he was placed, as the son of Lady Dunmelraise's dearest friend, and her own *protégé*), on recalling his descriptions and praises of Lady Adeline when they met at Restormel, he thought he saw a confirmation of his worst fears. What, he asked himself, could induce a young man to seek so lonely

112

and retired a situation but love? And Lady Dunmelraise he thought must have approved his views, or she would not have suffered such an intimacy to subsist, even though as her friend's child she received him under her roof; at least it was evident that she chose to give her daughter an opportunity of turning her affections from that quarter to which they had been originally directed. Adeline's letters, too, so equable in their expression of calm content, so lavish in Mr. Foley's praise, so minute in her detail of his way of thinking and manner of feeling, showed that had she not been more than commonly interested in him, she could not have thus busied herself with analysing his character.

"It is clear," he said, "Adeline does not love me; and her mother is no longer anxious in consequence that our union should take place!" While this idea prevailed he was desirous immediately to break off the engagement; formed a thousand plans for doing this, in such a way as to appear disinterested and honourable in their opinion; and worked himself up to a belief, for the moment, that he was only acting with that refinement and generosity due to his own feelings as well as to Lady Adeline's, by losing no time in putting this resolve into execution, and then she would be free. But for himself, would the same step afford him the same advantage? Would his heart be really free? were there no strong ties that bound him to Adeline? no habit of attachment formed in his breast, though she had broken through the one, and apparently could never have cherished the other? Would he, in short, be free, though she were? Could he turn the current of his affections at once towards another object; could he accept the heart, even were it her's to bestow, of the person who had shewn such an interest in his welfare; of one whose beauty was enhanced by the deep expression which played over her features—whose manners, talents, character, were alike formed—could he make her his wife? Again he paused at that title—it had never been associated with any save Adeline, and when coupled now with another, it made him start from his own thoughts, as though he were guilty in indulging them.

Struck at this idea, and with the conviction of what would be the state of his own mind were he indeed at once to let Lady Adeline loose from her engagement, his feelings and his reasonings took another course.

"Should I be justified," he asked himself, "in the steps I am proposing, without further proofs of Adeline's inconstancy? My surmises perhaps have ground sufficient, but something more than surmise is due to her. It is true, I am told I shall never be happy with her," (and he shuddered as he repeated the words to himself); "but I very much doubt if ever I can be happy without her. My own conduct, too, lately—what has it been? Has it not carried with it proofs of coldness and neglect? Why should I expect to receive that constant and ardent devotion, which I have shewed no anxiety to retain; and what, on my part, has occasioned this passive indifference? Has it not been a growing partiality for the society of another—and was *this* Adeline's fault?" He dwelt on this idea for some moments, and his self-reproaches were painful. Then again he thought, allowing that all is as it was between us, that she loves me in *her* way, and I her in mine, is that enough to constitute lasting happiness? "*No, it is not.* I should loathe the insipid homage of daily duties pointedly fulfilled, and weary of a mind which had not sufficient energy to think for itself. If I saw that my wife did not enter, from a similarity of tastes, into my occupations and pursuits, I should feel no satisfaction in her doing so to oblige me; and I certainly have already observed, that Adeline's habits, and even her principles, have led her to a life of monotonous tranquillity and insipid cares."

And here again Lady Hamlet Vernon's words recurred to

114

him with tremendous power. Would it not then, after all, be more noble to set her free from an engagement, which would fail in producing the happiness that they both had been led to expect? He mused with painful intensity as his thoughts rested on this idea; but in the exercise of analyzing, comparing, and combining these various views of his situation, his mind was imperceptibly drawn to the single subject productive of them—his early attachment to Adeline; and he fell into a comparatively calm reverie—that species of calm, which dwelling upon *one* feeling generally produces, after the mind has been tossed about in various contending conflicts. His youthful and first affections, together with all the awakening recollections of early tenderness—the development of their mutual passion, ere yet they knew they were destined for each other—the happy prospect of bliss which had succeeded—all, all recurred to him, and revived the dying glow of attachment in his breast. He took out her picture from his writing-desk—gazed at the well-known features, yet thought he had never before been aware of their full and perfect charm, that union of intelligence with purity which is supposed to constitute the being of an angel, that perfect candour, mingled with quick perception, which this portrait conveyed, and conveyed but feebly in comparison with the original,—set the seal to his conviction, that no one could prove to him what Adeline had been.

In replacing the portrait, he lifted up some loose papers, and it chanced that the lock of Lady Hamlet Vernon's hair, which he had kept (and never since looked at) on the night when she had been overturned at his door, dropped from the paper. He could not but admire it; its glossy richness—its hue of gold shining through the depth of its darkness: it was certainly very beautiful, and he sighed as he laid it down. "What if, indeed, her words should be true, and how can they be *true* unless in one sense—in that of Adeline's loving another? It must, it must be so!" and this fatal conviction broke down once more all the fabric of happiness which a moment before he had erected: and in this revived frenzy of feeling he passed the night. It was broad daylight ere he could bring himself to seek repose, nor did he then till worn-out nature sunk in forgetfulness and sleep.

When he awoke the next day—for morning was far advanced—it was like one awaking from the delirium of fever. He felt exhausted, spent, as though a long illness had shaken his being—so much will a few hours of mental agitation unnerve the strongest frame. The more he tried to collect his thoughts and bring them to a final result, the less did he find himself capable of the effort; the energies of his mind seemed paralyzed; he appeared to himself to be under the influence of some spell which impelled all his actions in an opposite direction to his wishes, as in paralytic affections, the limb ever moves in a contrary motion to that which the sufferer would have it. He was perplexed, amazed, and saw no clue to guide him through the labyrinth. The object of all his wishes—she to whom all his views and plans had had reference from the moment he could feel at all—now appeared to have been almost within reach of his attainment, and yet, by some inimical power, was placed at a greater and more uncertain distance than she had ever been. Lord Albert was not a weak character: but who is not weak, while they admit passion, and not principle, to guide their conduct.

At length, after having run over the subjects of his last night's perturbed reflections, the decision to which he came was one, that feeling alone, unaided by moral and religious principle, was likely to conduct him to; and he determined to pursue a middle course, without making known his suspicions. He resolved to miss no opportunity of

116

observation, till he should either have his fears dispelled or confirmed concerning Mr. Foley. He argued, that to speak openly to Lady Adeline, would *not* be to know the truth. Perhaps she would not break from her engagement, from a motive of delicacy as a woman, however much she might wish to do so; and it was left for him to free her from a chain which was no longer voluntarily worn.

The more he reflected the more he thought the intricacy of the case required this delicacy on his part. She may not, he thought, be herself aware of the nature of the attachment she feels for me; compliance with her parent's wishes, habit, duty, the kindly affection of a sister's love, may be all that she has felt towards myself; and now, for the first time, she may experience the overpowering nature of love. This must be what Lady Hamlet Vernon alluded to; and if it is really so, I should mar her happiness as well as my own, by leading her to fulfil such a joyless engagement. Oh, if indeed Lady Hamlet Vernon has saved me from the wretchedness which a marriage, under these circumstances, with Adeline, must have produced, what do I not owe her—gratitude—friendship—He hesitated even in thought—he hesitated to pronounce the word love; but a glow of feverish rapture passed through his heart as he recalled Lady Hamlet Vernon's beauty, her fascination, her evident partiality for himself. Yes, I must sift this matter to the utmost; I must have irrefragable proofs of Adeline's unshaken truth; nay more, of my being the decided and sole chosen object of her truest affections: and in the interim I will see her frequently —see her in the world as well as in retirement—and not allow myself to be blinded by the specious veil which hitherto habit, perhaps, has rendered equally deceptive to both.

Could Lord Albert have known this to be the self-same decision that Lady Adeline and Lady Dunmelraise had come

117

to in regard to himself, it would have gone far to have settled his determination at once, and to have hastened a declaration which must have confirmed his union with Lady Adeline. The fatal security however of thinking that, under all circumstances, Lady Adeline would keep her engagement with him, whatever he might ultimately decide upon, made him the more apprehensive of owing her possession to any motive save that of pure attachment; and it may be also (for the heart is deceitful above all things) that, resting on this very security, he had allowed his feelings to betray him imperceptibly into an aberration from their natural channel, till at length he could not distinguish truth from falsehood, and would too certainly deplore his error when the remedy was past his power.

Under the false but specious reasoning, then, in which he now indulged, he strengthened himself in his determination to pursue the plan he had laid down, namely, of watching the feelings and conduct of Lady Adeline in silence, and of endeavouring to elicit from Lady Hamlet Vernon, in whose friendship and interest he placed a fatal but implicit confidence, some of the grounds upon which her mysterious words rested. With this decision he prepared to go to South Audley Street.

CHAPTER VII.

TRUE NOBILITY.

It must not be supposed that Lady Hamlet Vernon admitted to herself that she was the mover of *premeditated* evil. Impelled by violent impulse, it is true she hesitated not in adopting means of any kind to attain her wishes; for she invariably succeeded in reasoning herself, however falsely, into a belief that she had at least some apology to gloss over, if not to justify, the measures she pursued.

Whatever calm she had assumed in her late interview with Lord D'Esterre, she suffered in secret the most painful agitation: the violence she had done her feelings, in concealing the disappointment she endured on Lord Albert D'Esterre's leaving Restormel, and the restraint that those feelings had since undergone before she found a favourable opportunity of speaking to him, all contributed (when at length that opportunity at Lady Tilney's supper-party did present itself) to render their indulgence more overwhelming. When she returned home that night, the sleepless hours of suffering she passed were not less painful in degree than those in which Lord D'Esterre shared; with this difference only in their nature, that the anguish endured by him was of a varied and mixed kind; whereas the whole mass of Lady Hamlet's wishes were centred in an uncontrolled passion for him; a passion which, since she had allowed it to wear its undisguised character, she found a thousand plausible reasons for admitting to control her

119

every thought.

There was no cause, she argued, sufficiently strong in Lord D'Esterre's engagement with Lady Adeline to forbid the indulgence of her love for him; *she* had no relative duties to sway her conduct—she was her own mistress: and in the opinion of the world—*her* world at least—she would be justified, where envy did not bias the judgment, in endeavouring to form so desirable a connexion. However Lord Albert D'Esterre might have been ostensibly considered by the members of the exclusive circle as one of themselves, and however much they affected to deride and despise his principles and habits, yet as a man whose talents promised to shine in the senate, and whose interest was considerable, his actions were not, in fact, quite so undervalued, or so indifferent to the leading personages of that body, as they might on a cursory view appear to be. He was still, Lady Tilney thought, too young, in her political way of viewing every thing, and had not given sufficient proofs of firmness, as a party man, for any direct overtures to be made to him on that score. But in as far as regarded his admission, in the first instance, to society amongst her coterie, he owed that distinction to his youth, his personal appearance, and his high rank; to his youth especially, as fitting him to become, under clever tuition, an obedient satellite; and when his very attractive exterior and manners, which were at once dignified and original, were added to the account, it is not to be wondered that he was reckoned a person worth courting, and a character worth forming, which might be incorporated, in due time, as one of their own.

Still there was a probationary state to pass through before any one was actually admitted into the arena of that circle. Lady Hamlet Vernon, however, who from his first appearance had marked him with her peculiar approbation,

120

was very clear-sighted as to the views which might be formed of others respecting an appropriation of him to their own purposes; and she thought she perceived, almost from the first, in the politic and eager attentions of Lady Tilney towards him, as well as in those of her silent but not uninterested lord, some ulterior object in obtaining his favour and confidence, which she imagined might also turn to her own account, as affording herself means to acquire an influence over him of another nature.

It is surprising with what quick perception women will discover the most hidden sentiments of others, when they have the remotest reference to the object of their favour and predilection; and many a man owes his success in life to the unceasing, and perhaps unknown endeavours to serve him, of some devoted, and it may be, unrequited heart. Who will watch like a woman over those minute details, which swell the aggregate of greater means? Who can feel, as a woman can, those vibrations of circumstances which may enable her to seize upon favourable moments, those *mollissima tempora fandi,* when the current of success may be directed to the object of her wishes. Lady Hamlet was well skilled to do all this, and from the first of Lord Albert's appearance in the circle in which she moved, her most diligent attention was ever awake to all that concerned him. She perceived that whenever he was spoken of, the Tilneys were particularly cautious and guarded in giving their opinion; and she was not mistaken in thence arguing that they were aware he might become a man of high consequence, in every sense of the term, as well as in their own peculiar acceptation of it.

Lady Hamlet Vernon felt that in this they had not formed an erroneous view of him, for she read ambition in his character: and though the species of that quality of mind was certainly very different in Lord Albert and in herself, yet its general nature was no stranger to her, and she knew it to be too powerful a lever in human actions to overlook or disregard it in this instance. On the contrary, she determined to use it in behalf of her own views; and from this motive she dwelt with energy on the subject of Lord Albert's prospects for the future, while conversing with him at Lady Tilney's. She then found she was touching a master-key to open the secret recesses of his mind and feelings. In its very first application, she had found it more than answer her expectations; and the consciousness that the apparent harmony of her sentiments with his on this point, had established an interest in and obtained an influence over the very main-spring of Lord Albert D'Esterre's being, inspired her with the liveliest hope.

No mercenary views, it is true, no mean love of power for little ends, actuated her, but a violent and overpowering passion, which, however, was equally subversive of rectitude of conduct, since it was neither guided by principle, nor restrained by moral or religious control. It was not directly any selfishness of motive that impelled her to the course she was pursuing, for she would have gone blindly forward in any plan the most contrary to her interests, her habits, or her feelings, which promised to draw her into a union of sentiment with the object of her passion; but those who suffer themselves to be directed by such impulses, are under complete delusion respecting the estimate they form of themselves. Whenever passion obtains the mastery, the effect is equally certain; the wholesome freedom of a mind at liberty is gone; and when once enslaved, it becomes like a wave of the sea, tossed about in every direction the sport of winds, and is as liable to dash into ruin, as to use any power it may possess to beneficial purposes.

Whilst the fever of agitation swayed Lady Hamlet Vernon, she gave herself up in secret to the inebriating delight of dwelling upon Lord Albert's looks and words, during their last interview; she recalled the expression of his eyes, as he gazed at her while she was speaking; she still seemed to feel the pressure of his hand thrill through her veins, as when he received the ring she gave him in pledge of friendship; but as these intoxicating sensations subsided, she relapsed again into fear, lest she should have gone too far at first; lest any thing she had said or looked might have appeared too violent, too plainly have told the tale of her feelings, ere time had ripened the moment when their disclosure might be more in unison with his wishes. Then again she hoped that her agitation might have been attributed alone to the caution which she had ventured to give him respecting Lady Adeline; and that she gave him such caution, she trusted would have been ascribed to a friendly feeling for his happiness. "Yes, his happiness!" she repeated to herself; "for I could sacrifice my own to secure that boon for him. It is not from motives of jealousy that I did so warn him, for I could bear to see him the husband of another, providing that other were really worthy of him, one who would share in his views, his plans, his feelings; but to unite himself with a woman wholly unfit for him—a girl, a weak insipid girl, made up of puritanical observances and prejudices—no, I could not see him set the seal to his future misery by allowing him to remain in ignorance of a fact which is known to all the world except himself."

In this sophistical manner did Lady Hamlet Vernon argue herself into the belief that no selfish motive impelled her, but that she was acting a noble part, and as the end designed was good, the means she thought were so likewise. In flattering this belief, she recalled every look and gesture of Lord Albert D'Esterre, and she thought she had perceived that he entertained a feeling of jealousy towards Mr. Foley. "Perhaps," she said, musing on that point, to which she had not before given her full attention, "perhaps his jealousy is not without foundation. Why is Mr. Foley so much at Dunmelraise? The circumstance of Lady Dunmelraise's protection of him through life, is not sufficient cause. After all, why should he not marry Lady Adeline, if she likes him? It would be a union much more consonant with Mr. Foley's happiness (inasmuch as he would not care what were her ways of thinking) than it would be for the noble-minded, aspiring D'Esterre."

In this new point of view Lady Hamlet Vernon found another specious argument in favour of her own conduct, and her secret wishes; and if indeed this latter assumption of a fact were true, she would be doing a doubly generous action, in forwarding the wishes of her friend Mr. Foley, while she at the same time saved Lord D'Esterre from a step that would inevitably render him unhappy.

Such were the false reasonings with which Lady Hamlet Vernon justified her feelings and her conduct to herself, and under their sway, she awaited with the utmost anxiety and impatience for Lord D'Esterre on the following morning. But it was late before he came, and he was abstracted and silent when he did arrive; unlike the animated being whom she had witnessed speaking to her with such force and expression of lively feeling on the previous evening. The fact is, Lord Albert D'Esterre had been at Lady Dunmelraise's, where he had found Adeline alone; and as, in her converse and presence, there was a soothing calm, a persuasive assurance, even in her silence, of her perfect purity and truth, those feelings of jealous doubt and mistrust that had preyed upon him before his visit to her, had gradually subsided while under the influence of her immediate power. Above all, the interest she expressed for him, the alarm she declared she felt on beholding his haggard look, and suddenly changed appearance, awoke in his breast all those tender feelings which it was a second nature for him to cherish towards her.

He felt indeed that he could have laid his head on her breast, confessed his folly, and wept out his fault in having for a moment suspected her; "but then again," he thought, "it will be time enough thus to humble myself when I see proof that my suspicions are indeed groundless; and I shall not be acting up to my resolution, if I allow a moment of tenderness to put it out of my power to certify the truth of her's."

Mr. Foley's name was not once mentioned during his visit. Mr. Foley did not appear; and for the time Lord Albert D'Esterre felt happy. "We shall see," he said to himself, "if this fair shew is real; a short time will serve to prove its truth, and then my happiness will stand on a secure basis."

He took leave, therefore, of Lady Adeline with a mind much relieved, and having impressed her also with the sensation that he felt towards her, all he had ever felt; but no sooner did he quit her presence, than, with that waywardness of spirit, which is too often apt to embitter our best interests, he was impelled to call on Lady Hamlet Vernon, for the sole purpose, as he fancied, of gathering indirectly from her conversation a more clear insight into the subject of her discourse. But in her presence, he in vain endeavoured to lead her to it; she avoided all reference, however remote, to the cause of his inquietude, and when she touched on the topic of his public career in life, Lord Albert felt that it was done in so vague and wary a manner, as to afford him no clue whatever to what engrossed at that moment all his thoughts, and he involuntarily became silent, and manifested an indifference to all farther converse. When he arose to take his leave, if he was less happy than when he had left Lady Adeline, he was not conscious of any reason why it should be so; but that of which he could not fail to be conscious, was the sensation that a spell was spread around him, whenever he approached Lady Hamlet Vernon.

To her inquiries if he would join her circle in the evening, and if he were one of those invited to the water-party the following day, he answered with apparent indifference; and, with a doubtful half-formed promise to attend her in the evening, he left the house. He was bewildered and uneasy; dissatisfied with himself, and consequently with all the world; and Lady Hamlet Vernon was miserable on her part at witnessing his change of manner, and remarking the serious and preoccupied expression of his countenance, which seemed totally at variance with her wishes.

That evening Lord Albert dedicated to a few hours of quiet in his own apartments; but the habit, of any kind, which has once been broken through, is not so easily resumed; and in particular the power of sober application to serious pursuits is hardly by any man to be laid by and recovered at will. The mind which is suffered to float about, driven by the winds of chance, becomes unfitted for fixed attention to any one particular point; and the effort is painful which must be made before it can be brought to bear on reflective subjects, after having been suffered to follow the vague direction of the feelings, or the yet more debilitating influence of dissipation.

Lord Albert acknowledged this, as he had recourse to various books for amusement. His attention wandered; and now he was at Lady Dunmelraise's, now at Lady Hamlet Vernon's—but never was he on the subject of the leaves which he vainly turned over; and after an evening spent in vacuity, he felt as fatigued, and more dispirited than had he been deeply engaged in some mental effort. The consciousness of this lowered state of being was exceedingly uneasy to him. He was one who, for so young a man, had learnt thoroughly to know the value of time, and when it was thus utterly lost or misapplied, he could not forgive himself for the irreparable fault.

Lord Albert, too, had an impression fixed indelibly on his mind, that when we are not advancing we are retrograding in our mental or moral course of existence; and fortunately for him, he was yet keenly sensible to the reproaches of conscience. His determination at the moment, therefore, to redeem this heavy loss was salutary and sincere; and he felt a renovation in his whole being when he took his early walk next day to Lady Dunmelraise's, full of the good resolutions he had formed the preceding day. To be in the presence of Lady Adeline Seymour, was like being in the sunshine of spring. There was an habitual serenity about her, which seemed to animate all around her; every thing and every sentiment of Adeline's was in its right place—no one took undue precedence of the other; the harmony of her form and features was a true reflection of her happily disposed nature; but that nature owed its very essence and continuance to the great ruling feeling of her mind. Every thought, and every action, were immediately or remotely under the guidance of pious belief: the nature of her happiness could not be uprooted by any earthly power; she might suffer *anguish here*; but she had a secret and secure joy that those only know who, like her, fix the anchor of their trust on an hereafter.

Having spent the greater part of the morning in such society, Lord Albert tacitly acknowledged its superiority to that in which he had lately lived, and the invitation he received to dine in South Audley Street was eagerly accepted. The party which he found assembled at Lady Dunmelraise's consisted chiefly of her family,—Lord and Lady Delamere, their two sons and daughter, and a few other persons who came in the evening. Lord Delamere was a shy man, and his shyness had sometimes the effect of pride; but the estimable points in his character were of such sterling value, that his friends loved him with a zeal of attachment which spoke volumes in his praise; and he was looked up to by his family, not only as their father, but their companion: nothing could be more beautiful than the union which subsisted between them; nothing more truly worthy of imitation than the virtuous dignity with which they filled their high station.

Lady Delamere still possessed great beauty; and the charm that never dies, the charm of fascination of manner and of air, defied the inroads which time makes on mere personal beauty. She was one of those very few women, who unite to feminine gentleness the qualities ascribed to a masculine mind. At the time she married, her husband's affairs were so much involved, that nothing but the utmost self-denial could possibly retrieve them: and she entered into his plans of retrenchment with an alacrity and vigour, which proved her to be a wife indeed; not the play-thing of an hour, to deck the board, or gratify the vanity of the possessor, but a companion, a friend, a helpmate, one who in retirement possessed resources that could enliven and cheer the solitary hour: who knew she was loved, and felt she deserved to be so, with that security of honest pride, which the consciousness of desert never fails to impart in married life, and yet whose refinement and delicacy of feeling never lost the elegancies of polished manners, because there were no novel objects to excite a sickly appetite for admiration.

To please is certainly the peculiar attribute and business of woman, in every relation of life; and those who neglect to foster and keep alive this power, reject one of the greatest means which Providence has placed in their hands to effect mighty operations of good. But there is a false and spurious kind of pleasing which must not be confounded with the true. Every woman will know how to distinguish these in her own conscience. When the wish to please is a mere gratification of vanity, when it lives always beyond the circle of her own hearth, and dies as soon as it is called upon for exercise within domestic walls; then, indeed, it may be known for what it is: but when, as in Lady Delamere's case, this virtue shone most splendidly confined to the sphere of home, its price was above rubies; in short it might truly be said of her, "the heart of her husband doth safely trust in her."

At the time when Lord Delamere was in the greatest difficulties, he did not, as too many do, fly to a foreign country, to continue the life of self-indulgence which he could no longer maintain in his own; he did not make it an excuse for forsaking his patrimony, and the seat of his ancestors, that he could not live there in that splendour which he had formerly done; but with a spirit of true pride he said: "the land of my forefathers with bread and water, rather than banishment and luxuries." He made no secret of his poverty; and it was a means of clothing him with honour: for with patience in his solitude he found content, and with content all things. His self-denial enabled him to be generous to others: and the very act of living on his estates, gave bread to hundreds. Lady Delamere went hand in hand with him in all his plans; and they pursued, for some years, with untiring step, the path of duty which they had marked out.

Meanwhile, their family grew up around them, and every thing prospered—for a blessing went along with them: they were adored by their dependents; honoured even by those who hated them for their superiority; and with the occasional visit of a relative or friend their time flowed on, fruitful in its course, and fraught with real and substantial happiness.

But in this their retirement they were not forgotten. It is not those who are fluttering about their empty shewy existence in the sunshine of pleasure and splendour whose memories live longest, even in that very world they so busily court. All great and useful works are the fruit of retirement; all strength of character is formed, not in indulgence and prosperity, but in retreat, and under the grave hand of that schoolmaster Adversity. The corn is not ripened till it receives the first and the latter rain: neither is the moral character formed to its great end, till it has known the storms of adversity. The Delameres had now reaped the fruits of this earthly probation, and they shone forth with lustre, which could not be eclipsed by any tinsel splendour of mere outward grandeur. The children of such parents could not be supposed to be altogether different from themselves, for though there are anomalies in nature, it rarely happens that the offspring are not like either father or mother, still less that they are not ultimately influenced by the example of parents.

When Lord Albert D'Esterre found himself in this happy society, so different, and yet, as he acknowledged to himself in every passing moment, so superior to that in which he had lately lived, he felt as if he also were of another race of beings; a pleased sort of self-satisfaction took possession of him: so much are we affected by outward things, so much does the mind reflect the hues by which it is surrounded. Are these, he thought, the persons whose names I have been accustomed to hear coupled with ridicule or condemnation—are these the persons who are designated vulgar? Strange indeed is the misnomer! And that there were many in the same grade, whose characters shed lustre upon their high stations, many who constituted the true character of British nobles, was a truth that Lord Albert had not sufficiently considered; for where is there a body in any country more worthy of respect and admiration than the real nobility of our land? It is only to be lamented that the errors of the few, and the assumed superiority of the *ton*, should have given ground for a false estimate of those characters of solid worth, whose virtues and whose ancient ancestry reflect a mutual value on each other; and the moral tranquillity of whose lives is at once a dignified refutation of the depreciation of high birth, and the best confirmation of its real consequence. But the middling classes, those who envy their superiors, or those who would attain to a distinction in society to which they have no immediate claim, are too apt in these days to form a mistaken judgment, founded upon newspaper reports or the spurious publications of the day, in which much false representation is mingled with some gross truths, and the delinquency of the few ascribed to the conduct of the many. Nor is it these alone, who are thus led into an erroneous opinion. The public press produces a circulation of good and evil, of truth or falsehood, universally; and wherever the latter creeps in, there ought to be an antidote administered. It should not be suffered to smoulder and gain force till it produce some serious mischief.

It should be told that the few individuals, whose idle and trifling lives, and whose tenour of conduct lay them open to contumely and blame, do *not* constitute the great mass of English nobility. So far from it, they are persons whose lives differ as much from the general existence of their compeers, as does the life of one individual in any class from that of another. Vice is not confined to nobility because a few great names have sullied its brightness. It is a false conclusion to consider *them* as examples of their caste, any more than the man in inferior station, whose delinquency is proved, and who suffers the penalty of the law, is to be taken as a specimen of the people at large.

In the course of conversation at Lady Dunmelraise's dinner,

the ensuing drawing-room was spoken of. "I am one of those old-fashioned persons," said Lady Delamere, "who feel a real pleasure in the thought of going to court—for first, I shall have the gratification of seeing my Sovereign, and of presenting to him another branch of that parent stock, who are personally as well as on principle attached to him and to his house. And though, doubtless, there are many who share in these feelings, yet I will yield the palm of loyalty and zeal to none; and, in the second place, I do very firmly believe that, in as far as society goes, a drawing-room does much moral good. There are certain lines drawn, which are useful to remind persons in general, that vice is contemned, and virtue honoured; and there is a distinction, too, of time, and place, and situation, which is not yet laid aside; I heartily wish there were many more drawing-rooms than there are."

Lord Delamere fully agreed with his wife in this opinion—the young people did not giggle and whisper, "what a bore it will be," but coincided with their parents. Lady Mary Delamere too declared, that she thought there was no occasion better suited to shew off real beauty to advantage than the splendour of a mid-day assembly, where every thing conspired to give people an air of decorative style which they could not possess at any other public meeting. "What pleasure," she continued, "I shall have in going with my cousin Adeline, and gathering up all the stray words of admiration, which I am sure will abundantly fall in her praise. Do tell me, love," addressing herself to her in a half whisper, while the rest of the persons at table conversed on other matters, "do tell me of what colour is your dress, and how it is to be trimmed?"

"Really," replied Lady Adeline, colouring as though she had committed a crime, "I have not thought about it. All I begged of Mamma was, that it might be very simple, and, I

132

believe, of a rose-colour—for a rose is my favourite flower."

"Dear child," said the good-natured Lady Mary, "you must think about it now, for the day is drawing near, and I shall be so disappointed if you are not well dressed."

"You are very kind, sweet cousin, but if you only knew how very little I care about the matter;" and she laughed heartily at the idea of its being a subject of the least importance.

"But, Lord Albert D'Esterre," said Lady Mary, appealing to him as he sat on the other side of Lady Adeline, "you will interfere, will you not? You will not be pleased, I am sure, lovely as Adeline is, to see her a *figure* at a drawing-room."

"What sort of figure do you mean?" he asked, smiling.

"Oh dear! you know well enough what I mean—unbecomingly attired."

"I think," he replied, "that although some figures will always be admired, still there is no merit in disdaining the usages of society or the advantages of dress, and that the neglect of appearance may in a young person be produced by some causes which are not desirable." He looked fixedly at Adeline as he spoke, and she blushed very deeply; but answered with an unhesitating voice:

"I shall be always desirous of pleasing those I love, even in trifles; but I should be sorry that trifles occupied their thoughts."

Lord Albert was silent; he felt a kind of chill come over him, for the remembrance of Lady Hamlet Vernon's instructions recurred to him; and he thought he saw a species of puritanical pride in the general tenour of Lady Adeline's manner of thinking and speaking, which seemed to justify the observations she had made upon her character. Then again he feared, that in other points he might discover more reason still to be dissatisfied—points on which his vital happiness rested. He looked instinctively round the room; but the person who at that moment crossed his thoughts was not present, and he again wrapped himself up in that mood of suspicion, which is ever on the alert to seek out the object which would give it most pain; under this influence he returned to the subject of Adeline's presentation dress, and said, addressing Lady Dunmelraise:

"I am not particularly an advocate for splendid attire; but I am sure, Lady Dunmelraise, you will agree with me in thinking, that there is an affectation in going unadorned to a court, which is a sort of disrespect to the place."

"Indeed," said Lady Adeline, in her wild eager way, "I will not go to much expenditure on my dress, for I have a plan for doing some good going on, which will require all the money I can collect, and I should be very sorry to see mamma wasting her's on any thing which I so little prize as my court-dress."

Lady Dunmelraise only smiled, and replied, "We must all subscribe to Adeline's toilette, for she is the veriest miser on that score herself. However, Lord Albert, do not be uneasy, I think she will not disgrace us," and the pleased mother passed on to other discourse.

This tenacity of Lady Adeline appeared to be a confirmation of his suspicions; and when, in the after part of the evening, Mr. Foley was announced, Lord Albert lost all command over himself, and under plea of a bad head-ache, sat silent, that he might the better watch every look and motion of Lady Adeline and Mr. Foley. Turning every indifferent word and gesture into the meaning with which his jealousy clothed it, he fancied that they were certainly mutually attached. Whatever soothing attentions Lady Adeline shewed to himself, he imagined were put on for the purpose of deceiving him; and his manner was so cold and haughty, that she in her turn began to shrink within herself, and to wear an abstracted, and somewhat distressed countenance.

Under this impression, Mr. Foley, with his *doucereux* air, whispered Lady Adeline, "that he was sure she was ill," and asked her "to cast out the evil spirit by her sweet power of music."

"Do, my love," said Lady Dunmelraise, "sing that delightful duet, which is always charming, '*O Momento fortunato!*' and then I feel sure we shall be all love and harmony—shall we not, Lord D'Esterre?"

The chords of the piano-forte relieved him from the embarrassment of a reply, and he listened to the impassioned tones of *poi Doman, poi Doman l'altro*, ascribing to every intonation and every sentiment of her feeling voice the dictates of a passion for his supposed rival.

"That used to be a favourite of yours, Albert," said Lady Adeline when the duet was finished; "but I am afraid your head-ache prevents you from enjoying any thing to-night."

"I do not feel well," he replied shortly; "and lest my indisposition should in any way affect the pleasure of others, I will hasten away."

"Oh yes, you appear ill, indeed!" said Lady Adeline, fixing her eyes tenderly on his; "and, dear Albert, perhaps you had better go—the noise of company may be too much for you:" and she held out her hand to him—"Oh, if you are unwell, by all means go home," she repeated, with an anxiety of tender interest, that no one else could misinterpret to be any thing but genuine affection, but which to him seemed to spring from the desire of his absence.

"You shall be obeyed," he said, returning her look reproachfully; and at the same time reaching his hat, which happened to lie on a table beyond Mr. Foley, he almost rudely snatched it away, and with a celerity of movement that admitted of no courtesy to any one present, departed. Lady Dunmelraise called after him, "Lord Albert, do you dine here to-morrow?" But he heard not, or affected not to hear, and with the gnawing rage of blind jealousy darted into his carriage, and gave the order, "home."

Soon after the rest of the party broke up; and when Lady Dunmelraise and her daughter found themselves once more alone, their mutual silence proved that they both felt the strangeness of Lord Albert's manner of departure. But although the words were on Lady Dunmelraise's tongue to utter—"*he is capricious,*"—she restrained, and suffered them to die away in silence, determined that her daughter's own unbiassed judgment should form for herself that opinion of Lord Albert's character, which would soon now ultimately decide on her acceptance or rejection of him as her husband.

CHAPTER VIII.

OFFICIAL LIFE.

It may be recollected, that when Lady Glenmore returned from the water-party, she was cruelly disappointed at finding only a note from her husband. "How little," she thought, as she sat at her toilette taking off the dress which in the morning she had not despised, as having been approved of and admired by him, but which now she cast aside with disdain—"how little men know how to value the affections of a wife! I have been for many hours in what is called a gay scene, and during the whole of the time, I cannot recal one moment when Glenmore was not present to my fancy; but he, I dare say, on the contrary, has not given a wish or a sigh to me." She looked in the glass as she thought this, and although a tear dimmed her eye, vanity whispered, "ought this to be so?"

"I am at least *pretty*; young, no one can deny; yet I am neglected for a number of old stupid men, a dull political discussion. Oh, those vile politics! how I hate them. And when he comes home, he will look so grave, so preoccupied! Oh, I wish there was no such thing in the world as a House of Lords or Commons. Is life itself long enough for love?— and must dull, dry business, consume the hours of youth, pale his cheek, perhaps blanch his hair, his beautiful hair, for they say care has whitened the locks even in one night! how very terrible this is."—And she arose, and walked to and fro in her room, and listened to every carriage that rolled by—then she took up Lalla Rookh—read some of the most impassioned passages, and wished herself a Peri.

"I have but one wish," she said, "that wish is to be loved as I love."—Poor Lady Glenmore! this beautiful phantom of a young heart is, nevertheless, in the sense in which she framed it, a mere deceit. Love such as her's does *not* grow by feeding on; there is a strength of character, a consciousness of self-dignity, the duties of a rational being, above all, the duties of a Christian, which must be cherished and understood, before any lasting fabric of happiness can be built on love. This was never more proved than in the restless impatience, the miserable (for such hours to such minds are miserable) anxiety and disappointment, which converted minutes into hours, and hours into ages, before Lord Glenmore returned. As she foresaw, when he did come, though he pressed her with almost rapturous tenderness to his heart, and inquired with trusting fondness at her party, hoping she had been well amused, he was himself so exhausted and harassed by business, that he professed himself unable to talk. "Why did you sit up for me, dearest?" he asked; "you will fatigue yourself uselessly; and I must really insist in future that you do not do so. At least, if you had been *amusing yourself*, I should, not be so sorry; but as it is, really Georgina, love, you must be better behaved in future—but why did you not go to the supper?"

"I came home to see you," she answered in a tremulous voice. Lord Glenmore chided her lovingly, and assured her that he had not less anxiously desired to return to her; but he said, smiling,

"You know you have the advantage over our sex, for *your business* is love—but our *business* is a matter apart from that gentler care. I long to tell you, my sweet Georgina, all that has interested me this day, and I think you will share in my satisfaction; but I am really unequal to enter into the details at present: to-morrow, love, you shall know all." Lady Glenmore only sighed; but with the sweet docility of her nature, never questioned his will, and his being with her constituted in fact all she cared to know. The truth was, that certain changes in the ministry had long been talked of, and on that morning overtures had been made to Lord Glenmore to take on himself an important office. The whole of the morning had been occupied in settling preliminaries, and ascertaining the sentiments of these public men with whom he was to act: for Lord Glenmore was a conscientious man, and would not mount a ladder, which he intended afterwards to cast down. It was not place he sought, but power, for purposes alike good and great. He felt within himself a capacity for the honours and distinctions he aspired to, and knew on principle the responsibility which attends success in such measures.

One of the first persons, whom he considered to be a man of inflexible integrity, and whom he wished for as a colleague in office, was Lord Albert D'Esterre; and since the situation which he had himself received threw several appointments into his own hands, Lord Glenmore lost no time in writing him the following note:

"MY DEAR D'ESTERRE:—I think that I shall not be making a proposal unacceptable to your wishes, or in discrepancy with your future plans, when I announce to you that I have accepted the office of — —. The official appointments immediately connected with it of course become mine, and it would afford me the greatest satisfaction in my arduous undertaking, to have one possessed of your talents to aid me in the performance of its duties. Would you accept the office of under Secretary of State in my department? I need not express my ardent hope that you will consent. You know that our views of public matters coincide thoroughly—let

139

me therefore hear from or see you as soon as possible.

"Your's ever most truly,

"GLENMORE."

After despatching this note, Lord Glenmore sought his wife, and entered into an account of what passed the previous day; he spoke of the increased expediency that would ensue of her living very much in society, whether he could himself be present with her or not; and added, that she must not allow any fears or mistrust, either of herself or him, to lessen the pleasure which it was natural, at her age and with her charm of person, she should derive from the homage around her.

"It is not mistrust, dearest Glenmore, that makes me feel joyless in your absence, for what can I fear?—it is true that I am uninterested in every thing, when you are not by to share my pleasure; but indeed you quite mistake me, love, if you suppose that I am not all confidence in you. And as to myself, what is there that can be for a moment dangerous to my peace, when all my interest, all my wishes, are centred in your love?"

"My own best Georgina," he replied, pressing her to his breast, "be ever thus, and what can I wish for more. But, love, mark me—you are now no longer the girl, whose duties were centred in passive obedience to her relatives, and whose recreations were the innocent, but trifling pursuits of girlhood; you are the wife of a man who is become a servant of the public—whose high cares must necessarily debar him frequently from the enjoyment of those domestic pleasures which a less busy or responsible life might allow. It is now become your duty, love, to feel your own consequence in his —to play *your* part in the scale by which his actions must be measured, and to be aware that many will court you from

140

an idea of your being wife to a minister, who would not for your own sake alone, perhaps, have thought of you; while others who previously courted you for the charm of your presence and the beauty of your outward shew, will now doubly affect your society, and endeavour, it may be, to use your influence to undue purposes. All are not pure and single-hearted like you, my dearest, and these cautions, believe me, are not given as to one whose worth I doubt, but, on the contrary, to one whose very ingenuousness and worth may prove a snare to her. In all that concerns mere knowledge of the world I recommend you to look to Lady Tenderden and Lady Tilney; they have passed creditably through the busy throng, and are certainly in all respects fashionable, and bear a high consideration in the estimation of the London world. You cannot do better, then, than to shape your course by their's in respect to what the French call *conduite*; and to the dictates of the heart, and moral duties, I refer you to your own and your excellent mother's."

Lady Glenmore scarcely knew why, but her heart swelled almost to bursting while her husband spoke thus to her; and it was with difficulty that she restrained the tears which seemed at every moment ready to overflow. The truth was she dwelt upon his first words, his declaration that his newly acquired honour would debar him from the pleasures of home society; and she looked up timidly as with tender accents she asked, "whether she was doomed now to be always absent from him."

"I trust not, dearest; at all events, you know my best and fondest interests are centred in you, and you would, I am sure, consider your husband's advantage and glory to be of value to you, even though these were obtained by the sacrifice of his company."

She said "yes," but *felt* decidedly, that had she spoken the truth, the "yes" would have been "no."

Lord Glenmore received several notes, and with a preoccupied air which prevented his observing the melancholy depicted on his wife's countenance, he snatched a hasty embrace, and was hurrying away, when looking back he said, "Remember love, not a word of this to any one, even to your mother. A few days will release the restraint I put upon your tongue," he added, smiling; "but in you I expect to find the *wonder*, that a woman can keep a secret; — in all things, I believe in, and trust you. Adieu, love, adieu." And he was gone.

That which would have pleased a vain woman, and gratified an ambitious one, fell only like lead on the young Georgina's heart.

"So," she said, sinking down in a chair, "I am a minister's wife. And am I the happier? Far, far from it; I am seldom now to see my husband, and when I do, the concerns of the public are to form our consideration and discourse; whereas, hitherto, in the short sunshine of our marriage, ourselves, our mutual hopes, our own dear home, have constituted all our care; and I fondly trusted, perhaps foolishly hoped, would have continued to do so. What a desolating change! But he says I must prepare for it; and since it is his will that thus it should be, I will endeavour to hide the mournful feelings of my heart. My dear mamma shall not see that I have wept either, for she will, perhaps, ascribe my tears to my husband's temper, and that would be worse still." So saying, she roused herself from the despondency into which she had fallen, bathed her face, called up smiles which were *not genuine* for the first time in her life; and, having re-arranged her dress, she said to herself as she cast a glance at her mirror, "Am I not now metamorphosed into the wife of a minister?" Just as she was preparing to ring her bell for her carriage, Lady Tenderden arrived.

"How well you are looking, *la belle aux yeux bleus*," said Lady Tenderden, kissing her: "there certainly never was any body who had the azure of the skies so exactly reflected in her eyes." This might be true; but it certainly was not true that she was looking well. To a vague answer given by Lady Glenmore she made no allusion; but looking at her very fixedly, so fixedly that it made her colour deeply, Lady Tenderden said, "Yet methinks something more than usual has occurred—is the report true?"

"What report?"

"Nay, now, do not make the *discreet*, for by to-morrow it will be in the newspapers. Come, tell me, your friend, am I not to wish you joy?"

"Of what, I may ask you in return, Lady Tenderden, for I can sincerely answer, that no increased cause of joy has befallen me, that I know of." This was said so very naturally, that her interrogator was posed. Judging by herself, Lady Tenderden conceived it impossible that the report of Lord Glenmore's having accepted a high office in government, which would have been the envy of so many, should be true; or else she thought the little lady must be more silly than she ever believed her to be. She went on, nevertheless, to sound Lady Glenmore in various ways, expecting to make out something relative to the subject; but Lady Glenmore's calm indifference totally foiled her, as she herself afterwards confessed; and she set it down in her own mind that for the present she could not be of any particular service to her, or derive any more reflected lustre from her, as being the friend of a woman whose husband was in power.

How the simplicity of a genuine character confounds the pertinacity of a keen worldly mind! Lady Tenderden was completely at fault: when another visitor, who came much on the same errand, afforded an additional proof of the truth of this observation. Lady Tilney came up to Lady Glenmore, and after the first salutation, entered with all her energy and eloquence upon politics; inveighing against government measures, and hoping that now a man of more liberal principles had come in, some change of *measures* at least would be adopted. Lady Glenmore sat abstracted, and began arranging her embroidery frame; seeing that there was no chance of Lady Tilney's speech coming to a conclusion:

"Well, my dear, and now," the latter said, "you will really have a part to play: how I envy you! What interest—what endless business will devolve on you! Were I you, I would propose to Lord Glenmore to write all his private letters for him; by this means you know you would be *au fait* of all the state secrets, and could, in a great measure, guide things your own way. You write rapidly, I believe; and your hand is not bad; it wants a little more character perhaps: but you know there is the man who advertises to teach any hand-writing. I do assure you he is excellent—I tried him myself, and a very few lessons from him would teach you to give your writing the firm diplomatic air—and you would quickly learn that significant style which means nothing; and by which, should any thing occur to make you change your mind (Lord Glenmore's, I mean), you could twist the phrase into another meaning, suitable to the occasion. I am sure I am always for decision and truth; but in certain cases prudence and caution are necessary; and therefore these resources are requisite to be observed in diplomatic writing. If you look back, you will always see it has been so in all ministers' letters."

Lady Glenmore, who had sat silent hitherto, now conceived herself obliged to speak, and replied, "that she knew nothing

144

of diplomacy, except the name; that every thing of the kind always made her yawn, and she hoped she should never have to copy any letters of business for any body." Lady Tilney in her turn stared, and observing that Lady Glenmore was very young, she said: "Well, but at all events you will be delighted to see your name perpetually with all the people in power; and to hear them say, that is the minister's beautiful wife! and the honours of your husband, at least to any one so domestically inclined, must be a great delight."

"I do not want Lord Glenmore to have any more honours than he has, for my own sake; but whatever pleases him will certainly please me."

"Oh, oh! so then you do confess it? and he *is* minister for — —"

"I am happy to hear it, if it really is to confer all the honour you seem to think upon him. But I wish you would tell me what *you* mean, Lady Tilney, for I do not quite understand you." There was a sort of real *not caring* about Lady Glenmore, which deceived Lady Tilney, as it had done Lady Tenderden. It was a thing so totally out of Lady Tilney's calculation that any one should not be enchanted at such a situation, that she was persuaded either that the fact was not so, or that Lady Glenmore did not know that it was the case.

Just as this inquisition had ceased, a servant entered with a few lines written in pencil on a card, which he gave to Lady Tenderden: they were from Mr. Leslie Winyard, to say, that having seen her carriage at the door, and having something very particular to communicate to her, he requested ten minutes' conversation, if he might be allowed to come up. Lady Tenderden remembered Lady Glenmore's former scruples about receiving him, but determined to overcome them.

"*Chère ladi,*" she said, "you must positively, notwithstanding the fear of Lord Glenmore, allow me to see Mr. Leslie Winyard; I will take all the *imminent* risk of the danger upon myself; and besides, you know, visiting *me* is not visiting *you*." Lady Glenmore looked exceedingly distressed, and said, "If you want to speak to Mr. Leslie Winyard, why can you not speak to him in your carriage?"

"Oh! that is so uncomfortable. Besides, Lady Tilney, I appeal to you, was there ever any thing so strange as Lady Glenmore's refusing to let Mr. Leslie Winyard come up stairs to see me, merely because *le tiran de mari* does not approve of morning visits from gentlemen?"

"Pho, pho," said Lady Tilney, "he was only joking, and that dear little good Georgina thought he was serious." Then turning to the servant who was waiting for orders, "Shew Mr. Leslie Winyard up stairs directly," commanding, as she always did, or tried to do, in every place and every person. In a few minutes Mr. Leslie Winyard made his appearance; and having paid his compliments to Lady Glenmore and Lady Tilney for some little time, he then stepped aside with Lady Tenderden, and after conversing together, apparently engaged on a most interesting subject, they returned to the other ladies, and he entered into general conversation with his usual light and amusing anecdote. At length, however, Lady Tilney arose, saying to Mr. Winyard, "well, notwithstanding your *agrémens*, I must go, for I have a hundred things to do." Lady Tenderden echoed this declaration, and they both went away, leaving Mr. Leslie Winyard, who seemed determined to sit them out *en tête-à-tête* with Lady Glenmore.

The consciousness that any thing has been said on any subject, always creates in an unartificial mind an awkwardness when the predicament that has led to the discussion really occurs;—and Lady Glenmore experienced this painfully. Every instant the sensation became stronger, and, of course, was not lost to the observation of her companion, though he affected not to perceive it; and by dint of feigning ignorance, and talking on indifferent subjects, he arrived at bringing her into the calm and comfortable frame of mind he had in view, one in which she would feel *le diable n'est pas si noir*; and this he effected with his usual address, till he evidently saw that she was rather diverted than otherwise by his conversation.

He then led the discourse to music, and entreated her once more to sing the *Sempre più t'amo* of Caraffa. She readily agreed, and their voices were in beautiful and thrilling unison when the door opened, and in came Lord Glenmore. His wife suddenly stopped, and rising from the instrument, looked abashed. Lord Glenmore, with the manners of a man of the world, addressed Mr. Leslie Winyard, regretted that he had interrupted the music, declared that he had some letters to write, and prayed him to finish the duet. But Lady Glenmore tried in vain to recommence singing—her voice faltered, her hand trembled, as she touched the keys—her eyes wandered to her husband with an expression of inquiry and uneasiness; and Mr. Leslie, too much the man of the world, and too much skilled in his *métier* to push matters at an unfavourable moment, declared that he was exceedingly sorry, but found himself under the necessity of going away, having an appointment on business which he could not put off. Apologizing, therefore, to Lord Glenmore, to whom he always took care to pay particular deference, for not being able to remain, he hurried out.

Lady Glenmore hastened with considerable trepidation of manner to explain to her husband how it had chanced that he found her singing with Mr. Leslie Winyard; but Lord

Glenmore seemed more deeply engaged in thinking of the letter he was perusing than of what she was saying, and only looked up smilingly in her face, and said, "My dear love, why are you so agitated about such a trifle?"—"Is it a trifle?" she said: "well, then, I need not care, and am quite happy again." She kissed his forehead; and further discourse was prevented by a servant's entering, to inform Lord Glenmore that Lord D'Esterre requested to see him if he was disengaged. Lord Glenmore immediately desired that he might be shewn into his private apartment; and at the same time gave orders that no one else might be admitted except the persons whose names were on the list; then pressing his wife's hand tenderly, but evidently much preoccupied in mind, he left the room.

"Is it possible," thought Lady Glenmore, looking after him —"can this be *my* husband, who so lately appeared to have no thought save what we mutually shared? and now we seem suddenly cast asunder: different interests, different hours, different societies, all seems to place us, as if by magic, apart, and to divide us from each other. He too, who dwelt so particularly on my not receiving morning visits from young men, now seems to think it is become a matter of indifference, or rather not to think about it at all. Has power then changed him so quickly? What a horrible thing power is!—how it transforms every thing into its own heartless self! Surely, surely, it is the most miserable thing in the world to be a minister's wife!" To dissipate the melancholy she felt, she ordered her carriage, and proceeded to visit her mother, who she found was ill, having caught cold in coming out of the Opera.

"Why did you not inform me of your indisposition before, dearest mamma?—I would have been here early?"

"I know, love, that you would not have been remiss in any kindness; but when a woman is married, her first duty is to her husband; and I fancy," she added, smiling, and implying by her manner that she knew more than she would exactly say; "I fancy Lord Glenmore will occupy more of your time than ever, dear Georgina, if what is reported be true."

"I am sure he will never prevent my coming to you, under any circumstances; but really he has so much business, that I see less and less of him every day."

"Indeed!" said Lady Melcomb, looking rather blank. Fortunately for both parties, Lord Melcomb came in from his morning walk, with a countenance even more bright and cheerful than was his wont. "So, my love," he cried, "I fear you must now be no longer my little Georgy, if the current news be true, I must look at you in a new light— eh?" and he examined her countenance.

"I am very sorry to hear that, dearest papa; I was so happy in the old one, that nothing can make me wish to change in your eyes."

"Come come, love, tell us now, has Lord Glenmore accepted the appointment of — — or not?"

"Whenever he tells me to say that he has done so, I shall certainly, my dearest papa and mamma, make you the first to be acquainted with the event."

"Well, Georgina, I see how it is: you need not say more, for you are already quite diplomatic in your mode of answering. But you are right, my child: whatever confidence your husband reposes in you, you ought to regard it as sacred;" and Lord Melcomb changed the subject like a good and a sensible man, who wishes really that his child should prove a good and faithful wife. "You have given the best earnest any girl can give," he said, "my sweet Georgina, of being an invaluable treasure to your husband, by having first been such to your parents; and the obedience you paid us should now be implicitly transferred to Lord Glenmore. The woman who has not learnt obedience, is likely to be very unhappy: for it is surely one of the first duties in every sphere of a woman's life. You know the lines, that I have so often repeated to you, and I am sure you practise them, my own Georgina, as forming the great golden rule to be observed by a married woman: one who

"'Never answers till her husband cools;
    And if she rules him, never shows she rules.'

"But when I say obedience, I do not mean that slavish obedience, which in matters of conscience must remain a question for conscience to decide; I mean that system of gentle acquiescence in all the minor motives of life, which can alone render the domestic circle a circle of harmony."

Lady Glenmore assured her father she had not forgotten, and never should forget his excellent lessons; and that every thing which he had recommended her to do, she invariably called to mind every night and morning. Lord Melcomb had, during a very busy life, acquitted himself under all circumstances with credit both abroad and at home, and if he had leant to the despotic side of governing in his own house, he had done it with so much gentleness as well as firmness, that no one felt inclined to consider the yoke heavy. His daughter had never even felt it could be so, for she was by nature and inclination a docile gentle being, leaning upon those she loved with implicit confidence for guidance and support. It was at this particular moment more than usually sweet to her to be in the society of her parents, and she promised that if Lord Glenmore were engaged in the evening, she would bring her work, and instead of passing the *then* dull hours at home, find a sweet solace with them; they were a happy family, united in the bond of the strictest union, and even at a temporary parting felt pain, in proportion as being together gave them pleasure; but it was time for Lady Glenmore, she said, to go home, and they separated.

The interview between Lord Glenmore and Lord D'Esterre that morning had passed to their mutual satisfaction; their general opinion of public affairs, and their views of domestic happiness were too similar for them not to draw together;

151

and yet there were points of difference in their character, which tended to keep alive an awakening interest, and render the one more necessary to the other; but in regard to the great question then agitating the public mind, Lady Tilney was quite mistaken in her ideas of his principles, which were at variance in many respects with what she called *liberalism*.

The fact was, the minister of the day, having discovered that those whom he had allowed to continue in office, on agreed and well-defined principles as to the line they were to pursue in their political conduct, were acting out of the pale of their engagements, and forfeiting the pledges given to himself; consequently, with that decision of character, and straightforwardness of conduct, which formed the leading feature of his life, he availed himself of the first favourable opportunity of breaking off a connexion with men, whose moral complexions were so very unlike his own. Well knowing how vast were his resources, he sought among the rising nobility of England (who, take them altogether, form perhaps, a body more talented, and more patriotic than any other nation in the world) for that support and coadjutancy which the emergency of the times demanded, in order to maintain the constitutional rights of the nation. Lord Glenmore was one of these, and amongst the parties whom he, in his turn, named as being those he wished should co-operate with him in his individual department, Lord D'Esterre stood pre-eminent. This happy nomination met at once with the entire approbation of the minister, whose discernment was as penetrating, as it was prompt and decisive.

Lord Albert, it may be, in his acceptance of office, was not influenced alone by political views. He felt that, in the uncertain and agitated state of his mind, some great and commanding power for exertion was necessary to him; some influential weight of sufficient magnitude to poise the fluctuations of a mind, whose energies he was conscious were wasting themselves in a diseased state of excitement. He thought that by engaging in a political career, where the duties imposed were of an imperious and absorbing nature, he should best find that refuge against himself which he deemed it wise to seek. Men in such cases have most indubitably great advantages over women; many a noble career lies open to them. When they are oppressed by any woe of a private nature, they may in the exercise of their powers find arms against a sea of troubles; but women have only one great lesson to learn, greater still perhaps if duly entertained—to suffer resignedly.

Lord Glenmore and Lord Albert prolonged their discussion to a late hour—so late that Lord Glenmore pressed him to remain and dine. "We have no company to-day," he said, "and Lady Glenmore will excuse your toilette." The invitation was too acceptable to be refused, and they passed into the drawing-room, where they found Lady Glenmore all smiles and beauty; for the idea of enjoying her husband's company had again restored her to her wonted placid happiness.

The conversation took that happy course which it ever does when similarity of tastes directs the subjects; and as the minds of these young men were not only of a superior cast, but their manners too formed on that refined model which, when it is accompanied by intellectual power, gives grace to force, their social intercourse was truly such, as one likes to think is the sample of a high-born, high-bred British nobleman.

Lady Glenmore listened with no insipid mawkish indifference, even to matters beyond her ken, and the remark she ventured now and then to slide in was one that bespoke a diffident, but not deficient understanding. A delighted glance of approbation occasionally escaped from Lord Glenmore, in homage to his wife, and as Lord Albert beheld this married happiness, he could not help sighing, as he thought "such might have been mine;" and he almost unconsciously drew a parallel between Lady Glenmore and Adeline, in which he did not deceive himself in giving the decided palm to the latter.

When he was preparing to depart, he found it was so late that he drove home; but when there, the same incapacity to settle himself to any occupation which he had before experienced, returned, and he fancied that he might yet be in time for an hour of the ballet. So he ordered his carriage, made a brief toilette, and drove to the Opera-house. "It is too late," he thought, "to go to South Audley Street; I shall disturb Lady Dunmelraise;" but yet the idea that he had not called upon her that day haunted him painfully.

Arrived at the Opera, he walked in, and hearing, as he passed the pit-door, a favourite air sung by Pasta, he made his way through the crowd, obtained a tolerable place, and was listening intently to the music, when he was accosted by Mr. George Foley. The recollection of what he had suffered the previous evening came freshly to his feelings, like a dark dense cloud, obscuring every other idea. Mr. Foley, either not seeing, or not choosing to see, the coldness of his reception, pertinaciously kept up a conversation with him on various subjects, precisely in that quiet and self-satisfied manner, which is so insufferable to a person under feelings of irritation. Nor did Mr. Foley cease talking till he suddenly turned round, and saw some one in the boxes, to whom he nodded with much apparent familiarity of interest. Lord Albert mechanically turned his head also, and beheld Lady Hamlet Vernon—who kissed her hand to him; and both of them, as if by mutual consent, proceeded to join her. She was but just arrived, having been at a dinner at the

154

Leinsengens, she said, and her face was lit up with more than ordinary animation as she greeted them on their entering; then noticing to Lord Albert to take the seat next her in front of the box, she bent towards him, so as to whisper in his ear, "I heartily congratulate you; I have just heard of the arrangements at the Leinsengens where I dined, as I have already told you, and where I heard all the finest things in the world said of you, as I have not yet told you; but I assure you the generality of the persons there were, I really believe, for once sincere in what they said. But you do not express any satisfaction at this event yourself: why are you so exceedingly indifferent?" and her eyes spoke a language which was any thing but that of indifference.

"Because," he said, "I do not avow that the news you have heard is true. We must wait and see the event publicly announced, before one can have any feeling about it, one way or the other." Lady Hamlet Vernon continued to banter him on his cautious reserve for some time; but did not press the matter further, as she saw his dislike to being probed on the subject.

"Only remember," she whispered, "you have one friend, who enters into all your joys and sorrows, and feels every thing that betides you with a keen perception of interest." After some vain attempts on her part to unite Mr. Foley in a conversation with them, which she resumed aloud, he being perfectly aware that Lord Albert in fact engrossed her completely, took an early opportunity of withdrawing. Lord Albert remained till near the close of the ballet in earnest conversation with Lady Hamlet Vernon, interrupted only occasionally by chance visitors, who seeing the preoccupied air, and observing the thoughtful expression of Lord Albert, did not long obtrude themselves. He would probably have remained where he was till the entire end of the performance, had not a sudden movement in the box

155

opposite, attended with bustle, and some lady apparently fainting, caught his attention. He looked eagerly again, and in another minute recognized Lady Delamere, and thought in the reclining figure that he could trace a likeness to Lady Adeline Seymour. Hastily rising, he rushed out of the box, without making any apology to Lady Hamlet Vernon, or mentioning the cause of his very abrupt departure.

When he arrived at the opposite side of the house, he found his fears and conjectures true; and his heart smote him in an instant, as he figured to himself what Lady Adeline's feelings must have been, in seeing him occupied so long a time, and his attention so intensely fixed upon another, as he was conscious his had been on Lady Hamlet Vernon. Although Lady Adeline might not know who she was, yet the circumstance of his not having been near her all day, the reason of which she could not know, together with the fact which she saw, namely, that he preferred the society of another to her's, were all circumstances that struck him with self-condemnation, and his look, and manner, implied the full expression of tender penitence. But Lady Adeline was still insensible; she could not see, or observe, *what* his feelings then were at beholding her thus; but with Lady Delamere the case was different; he thought he read in her cold reception of his offered services, and the penetrating glance which she cast upon him, her complete knowledge of all that had passed in his mind relative to Lady Hamlet Vernon, and he shrunk confused from her gaze.

This, however, was neither a time nor place adapted for explanations; and, indeed, to whom was he to make them? To no one did he feel responsible but to Adeline; to no one he felt would they be satisfactory, save to Adeline. He knew her mind was truth itself, and so utterly incapable of deception, that she could not believe that any one would deceive her; he determined therefore to unbosom himself to her, and be forgiven. With these feelings, which were rapid and almost simultaneous in their effect, though language is slow in expressing them, he caught the sinking Adeline in his arms, and lifted her inanimate form into the corridor, where a seat being hastily taken from the box, he supported her, kneeling by her side. At this moment Mr. Foley appeared, breathless with haste, bearing some water and a smelling-bottle, which he proceeded to apply, whilst Lady Delamere aided him in his efforts to restore Adeline, and was assisted by several of their acquaintance who were passing by.

Lord Albert could only partially be of use, as one arm supported her; but with the other he tenderly pressed her hand as he bathed it in the water. Animation, after a few minutes, returned; she opened her eyes, and gazed vacantly; but in another moment her senses were fully restored; and on recognizing Lord Albert, she quickly closed her eyes again, and a sort of convulsive throb seemed about to make her relapse; but struggling to disengage her hand, which he let drop with an expression of sorrow and dismay, Lady Adeline made an effort to recover herself; and half rising, she turned to Lady Delamere, and said inarticulately, "I should like, dear aunt, to be taken home."

"Stop, for heaven's sake," cried Lord Albert D'Esterre, stepping forward, as if to catch her tottering frame; "wait till you are more recovered."

"No," she said; but speaking still as if to Lady Delamere, "I shall be better when I am at home; dear aunt, let me go." Lady Delamere, judging of Adeline's feelings by her own observations of the circumstances which she thought had caused her sudden indisposition, said coolly, addressing Lord Albert, "Thank you, Lord Albert, but Adeline is the best judge of her own feelings." Then turning to Mr. Foley, she asked him if he had seen her servants. He answered in the affirmative; and added, "the carriage will be up by this time certainly."

"Then," rejoined Lady Delamere, "have the goodness, Mr. Foley, to give your arm to my niece;" and she continued, with marked emphasis, "Adeline dear, I will support you on the other side." It was impossible for Lord Albert to mistake what this arrangement implied; his whole frame was convulsed, though he betrayed no gesture of suffering, but stood rooted to the spot, as his eyes gazed on her, walking away feebly between her two supporters, without thinking of following her; and then, by a sudden impulse, he rushed after her, and arrived at the door just in time to see Mr. Foley get into the carriage, after having placed the ladies in safety, and to hear the word "home" pronounced by the footman as they drove from the door of the Opera-house.

He mechanically turned round, and with an agitation of mind that allowed not of reflection, returned to Lady Hamlet Vernon's box. He sat down without speaking; and, gazing in vacancy, remained for some time like one in a deep reverie. Fortunately there was no one in the box but themselves; and though Lady Hamlet Vernon was quite aware of his situation, and partly guessed the cause, she was too deeply interested herself in the issue of the event to press indiscreetly into his feelings at that moment, but simply asked him "if he were not well?" "Oh, quite well," he replied; "only rather astonished.—It was,"—he stopped—seemed to muse again, and then he added to himself, "they went away together." Lady Hamlet Vernon's eyes filled with tears— (tears will come sometimes to some people when they are called)—she said, in a low voice, "I must always grieve for what gives you pain; but I have thought"—she paused.— Lord Albert fixed his eyes on her for an instant, as if he would inquire, "what have you thought?" but the latter, without appearing to deny that she *had* thought, at the same time added, in a hurried tone,

"Yet, my dear Lord Albert, let not my thoughts weigh with you; let not a momentary appearance alone decide on any measure which may influence your whole life; look dispassionately on appearances; sound them, sift them thoroughly, ere you allow yourself to act upon them." There was a gentle reason in these words, an expression of heart-felt interest in the speaker, which at the present instant was doubly efficacious in turning the current of his thoughts and feelings in favour of her who uttered them; and he gave way to a warmth of expression in his reply which was joy to her heart. Still she repressed the triumph she felt at this impassioned answer; and it was only when he handed her to her carriage, that the pressure of her hand spoke a tenderer language, which vibrated through his frame.

END OF VOL. II.

LONDON:
PRINTED BY J. L. COX, GREAT QUEEN STREET.

THE
COURT JOURNAL.

The whole impression of this new and popular weekly journal being now stamped, subscribers may receive and transmit it to their friends, POSTAGE FREE, throughout all parts of the kingdom.

THE PROPRIETORS of the COURT JOURNAL, with due acknowledgments for the highly gratifying reception their work has already met with, beg leave to point out to readers in general the advantages of their publication in its present improved form.

The occupations, engagements, and amusements of the higher classes of society had long required a record; they found it in the Court Journal. The fête champêtre, the sumptuous banquet, the concert, the soirée, the ball, the public and private habits of royal and noble life, those habits which give the tone to manners throughout the empire, were depicted with a freshness and accuracy hitherto unattempted; and, in all instances, with the most attentive avoidance of injury to personal feelings. It may be easily imagined that those details could not have been supplied from ordinary sources,—thus the connexions of the Proprietors afforded them peculiar opportunities, and many of the articles of the Court Journal were contributed by individuals, whose rank and fashion gave even a pledge at once for the good taste and the truth of their descriptions.

But something more was still required, to realize the original idea of the publication. It was hitherto the Journal of an elevated but exclusive class; the purpose was to render it available to all classes, retaining its anecdote, pleasantry, and spirit of high life, to make it the vehicle of intelligence of every interesting kind; the companion not only of the boudoir but of the breakfast table and the study, —a Journal in which not merely the woman of fashion might find the round of her engagements for the week brought gracefully before her eye; but the politician, the student, and the various orders of intelligent society might find the species of information suited to their purposes; to make the Court Journal a WEEKLY NEWSPAPER of the most improved and valuable nature.

For this object a Stamp was necessary, and the Proprietors did not hesitate to subject themselves to the serious additional expense, that they might give the public their paper in its complete state, feeling confident that the claims of the work to great popularity and extensive circulation would be duly estimated by the public at large.

THE COURT JOURNAL is regularly published every SATURDAY MORNING on a handsome sheet of 16 quarto pages, containing 48 columns, price 10d. and may consequently be received on Sunday in all parts of the country. Published for HENRY COLBURN, by W. Thomas, at the office, 19, Catherine Street, Strand. Orders are received by all Booksellers and Newsvenders throughout the kingdom; and those who desire to become subscribers are particularly requested to give their orders to the Bookseller or Newsman in their own immediate neighbourhood, as the best mode of receiving it regularly.

N.B.—Advertisements or orders sent from the country to the office must be accompanied by a reference for payment in London.